Bill Hayward

About the Author

JUSTIN TAYLOR was born in 1982. His fiction and nonfiction have been published by *The Believer*, *The Nation*, *The New York Tyrant*, *Flaunt*, the *Brooklyn Rail*, *n+1*, NPR, and *Time Out* (New York), among many other journals, magazines, and Web sites. In 2007, he edited an acclaimed short fiction anthology, *The Apocalypse Reader*, and guest-edited an issue number 24 of *McSweeney's*, for whom he produced "Come Back, Donald Barthelme," a symposium on the author's life and work. He is a regular contributor to HTMLGIANT: The Internet Literature Magazine Blog of the Future. Taylor lives in Brooklyn, and he is at work on his first novel.

EVERYTHING
HERE
IS
THE
BEST
THING
EVER

EVERYTHING
HERE
IS
THE
BEST
THING
EVER

stories

JUSTIN TAYLOR

HARPER ◖●◗ PERENNIAL

NEW YORK • LONDON • TORONTO • SYDNEY • NEW DELHI • AUCKLAND

HARPER ● PERENNIAL

FIRST EDITION

Designed by Justin Dodd

Library of Congress Cataloging-in-Publication Data is available upon request.

ISBN 978-0-06-188181-7

10 11 12 13 14   OV/RRD   10 9 8 7 6 5 4 3 2 1

This book is for Amanda Peters

So holy and so perfect is my love,
And I in such a poverty of grace,
That I shall think it a most plenteous crop
To glean the broken ears after the man
That the main harvest reaps. Loose now and then
A scattered smile, and that I'll live upon.

—*As You Like It*, III.5

I sang the way I still talk. Every song was the worst way I could think of to ask for what I did not yet know how not to want.

—Gary Lutz, *Stories in the Worst Way*

CONTENTS

EVERYTHING

HERE

IS

THE

BEST

THING

EVER

AMBER AT THE WINDOW
IN HURRICANE SEASON

By two o'clock the sky had gone to ash. Amber pushed a blond lock behind her ear, stray hairs glancing off a steel row of studs driven like garden stakes through the cartilage of her helix and lobe. Her other hand still held the roll of duct tape with which she'd reinforced the window, the glass marked now with a dull silver X. She looked around it, out at the world. She wore pre-faded jeans and a small tee shirt. Stylish, but not quite *in* style, the wardrobe alluded to punk rock, outlet malls, and other holdover habits from high school. A year later, when you saw her in her no-longer-quite-new skirt (the plaid one so short you kept catching glimpses of her white white underwear) she seemed like someone else altogether. You were all wet from having jumped into the aboveground pool. She gave you an old Misfits tee shirt and a pair of JNCOs to wear while your clothes dried, and you thought, *Oh, I remember Amber now.*

When she smiled her cheeks turned to waxed apples but she wasn't smiling there at the window. She was worrying that the oak tree might come through her ceiling, wood obliterating wood, like a miracle running backward.

In the glass, between the silver diagonals of tape, she saw her own ghost. She stared through the translucent creature and focused on the measly expanse of grass between her building and the deserted street, its shuttered shops and condemned strays. Beyond that there was only the storm. It was really going to happen. And you weren't there.

Your name was Patrick. You were still away, maybe out somewhere with your new friends or jerking off in some bathroom thinking about Marissa, who you never told Amber about, and who, you should never forget, I had before you did. I always wondered what you saw in her that I couldn't, what made her off-ness on for you, but mostly I was just glad she began stopping at your bedroom door and left my end of the hallway alone. She was an ugly drunk, which was part of it, I already had one of those in my life—but this isn't about Marissa, it's not about you, and I won't allow it to devolve into another damn soliloquy for Kim. This is about Amber, and the thing that wore away at us like waves beating beach sand until the day I kissed her and she liked it. We didn't tell you. It was ours. We could have fucked maybe twice before the remorse caught up with us. Do you suppose we did?

She was a weather freak, as you'll recall, crushed out on every forecaster, even the old fat ones. Late nights would dissolve into early mornings while she waited for her favorites, with their toupees and full-color satellite imagery. Sometimes I'd find her in the living room appraising the ten-day forecast with a sexualized eye not unlike the one I cast on her or you cast on whoever you weren't ignoring just then. The predictions were always dire. The animated projections repeated, over and over, as if scratched by a DJ. She tracked the progress of every named and unnamed storm.

She told me this one would be the worst and remain the worst for a while. That's why I picked it to tell about, whatever its name was or would have been. There's always a new worst; only tenure varies. I was eager to see the city pelted and drubbed.

But I wasn't there either. This picture of Amber at the window in hurricane season is a second-rate sketch, my little vision, an unfair summation of an era—a summer—we spent in grand subtropical poverty, sipping rum drinks so sweet they were almost sour and boasting that we were the people who did not listen to Jimmy Buffett. We listened to sad songs and the birds that haunted the oaks between the duplexes and low-rise apartments like the one Amber hadn't moved into yet. The one where you found her again.

Cars were rare and there were stars at night. We stood on the porch. On the sidewalk some genius had spray-painted EVERYTHING HERE IS THE BEST THING EVER and nobody from the city ever came to clean it up. I began to believe we were the secret owners of the world and everything in it: our shitty rental home; that one bar on Tenth that we liked; the whole state from the Alabama border over to St. Augustine, down past the Rat Kingdom all the way to Hemingway House and the beaches from which you can practically spit on Cuba. Amber would sleep in your bed, the window open, smelling the early summer and the last of you in the sheets. Hurricane season hadn't started. Every night was balmy. We'd make ridiculous breakfasts at all hours, bacon and pancakes, stacks and piles, heaps, and wonder how you were doing, if you would ever send for her or wash back up here or never call again, or what. She never did the laundry. Sometimes I wouldn't sleep for days.

IN MY HEART I AM ALREADY GONE

This was a long time coming." That's the first thing Uncle Danny says after he says the thing he took me aside to say: that he wants to hire me to get rid of his house cat, Buckles. We're out back, he's smoking. I wouldn't mind a smoke but I don't want to ask him for one. The sun is going down into the man-made lake with something not unlike majesty, and when I glance back toward the house (pool needs a skim) I can see Vicky and Aunt Amanda inside, finishing cleanup. Vicky collects the dishes and serving things, her mother washes them in that perfect way she has, Vicky dries, and they both put them away.

I have dinner with my uncle's family on Wednesday nights. They set a full table. With me here we are four, and sometimes I think of myself not as Vicky's cousin, but as her big brother. Not quite ten years between us. Sometimes my mother comes with me, but not usually. After a long day at work, she says, she'd rather have the silence than the company.

"You're sure about this?" I say to Uncle Danny. I am not surprised that he doesn't acknowledge my question. He is not a man who thinks aloud, but one who broods, then takes action. He probably made up his mind about how this conversation would go before I got here. I am tempted to raise objections just to hear the responses he's worked out, but the fact is that I don't object. I'm honored that he asked me.

Vicky is a good girl, her mother will tell you so, though if Uncle Danny is in the room when you are talking about this, he is likely to stay silent. He may look up from his paper, but he will keep his peace. She is fifteen, her dark hair streaked blond. She cuts her own bangs, a ragged diagonal like the torn hem of a nightgown. She is not allowed to date. Her braces, she thanks God, have come off. She wears band tee shirts procured for her by friends, souvenirs from arena concerts she is not permitted to attend.

The Watsons (one time I overheard Vicky on the phone with some friend: "God, I even have a boring *name*") keep a clean house. Amanda regularly vacuums and mops, but Buckles sheds and sheds. There is always a thin coat of fur on the furniture, tufts on the floor, even some in the air: a minor atmospheric condition. Sometimes you'll look toward a window and see a tuft headed earth- or couchward, caught in the AC slipstream, seeming almost to dance rather than fall.

•   •   •

Buckles is locked in the guest bathroom, mewling to be let out. For the past few weeks, no one knows why, Buckles has become "stressed out" (Amanda's term) and has started to throw up his food. The vet says there is nothing wrong with him. The summer is over, Vicky is in school again, and Amanda is now working. The cat is lonesome.

Amanda says she's started working because she is bored with being a housewife, now that her daughter doesn't need full-time mothering, but the fact is that Danny's business has been flagging. With everyone so busy, sometimes the cat vomit on the windowsill or under the couch will go unnoticed for days until somebody smells something and then finds the awful little pile of dried-up goo, the muted, autumnal reds and browns of their brand of cat food, garnished with white-gray sprigs of shed fur and some new-grown mold.

One time I was going to see a concert at the arena, a band that Vicky also wanted to see. This doesn't happen very often, us wanting to see the same band, so I offered to take her. "She can come with me and my friends," I told Danny. "I'll keep an eye."

"It's not that we don't trust *you*, Kyle," Uncle Danny said. "It's just that Amanda and I don't want Vicky exposed to that sort of influence."

"I see what you're saying," I said, "but if she already knows the music well enough to want to go to the concert—"

"Kyle," Uncle Danny said.

I had a better time without her, I'm sure, just getting fucked up and enjoying myself, but afterward I told her that I had tried for her, and gave her a shirt from the concert. I told her if her parents ever asked to say that one of her friends had gotten it for her. But her shirts, to her parents, are just shirts, vaguely offensive but not worth confiscating. They wouldn't know any one of those bands from any other even if they did bother to read the names, always ornate silver script on black, some red-filtered cluster of sullen, long-haired guys.

"Try it on," I said to her.

"Okay," she said, but then did nothing, only stared, as if waiting for something.

"Just face away from me," I said, "if that's what's bothering you," and noticed a little Orion's belt of pimples on the blade of one naked shoulder as she changed.

"You're not even going to name your price," Uncle Danny says.

I say, "I'm sure whatever you decide on will be fair. Besides, this isn't business, it's family."

"Good," Danny says. "That's good. You're a good kid, Kyle." He reaches into his pocket and takes out two keys on a ring. The fob is a little clown head with red circles for cheeks and a cone hat and it squeaks when I squeeze it.

Back in the house, over oven-warmed supermarket apple pie and bright yellow vanilla ice cream, Aunt Amanda talks about her appointment tomorrow. It won't be bad, and anyway it ought to be a quick visit, right? Everyone agrees. A few weeks ago she went in for a test, and Danny was grim-faced and Vicky went out of her way to be good. Tomorrow she goes for her results.

I ask Vicky how school is going. She begins telling about some especially unreasonable teacher of an otherwise enjoyable subject, then turns to Amanda. "I'm really sorry, Mom." Her doe eyes are defined by the mascara she used to hide in her bag and put on at school, but which Amanda has only recently convinced Danny is not inappropriate for a young lady. He still says she looks painted, but he's dropped any pretence of action. She is radiant, almost crying.

Desperate for another subject, Amanda asks me how *my* school is going, and I try to explain the concept of negative capability until she seems satisfied. I am pushing through the course with a solid C, which could even become a B if I ace the midterm, and in my heart I am not a student in junior college anyway. In my heart I have already left this miserable town behind for a place and future so bright with promise I cannot look directly upon it, which is maybe another way of saying that, though in my heart I am already gone, am calling my mother on her birthday or sending a Christmas gift to Vicky, I don't know where I'll go or how to get there.

When Vicky asks to be excused from the table, Danny says he will come by her room in a bit to check her homework. Toward the end of the last school year she slacked off and was not on the honor roll during the final quarter. She was grounded for the whole first month of her vacation. I told

Danny, privately, that I thought he was being too harsh. "It's the summer," I said, "and she's just a kid. My mom never grounded me for my grades."

"Yes," he said. "That's right."

"Danny, he's still crying in there," Amanda says, after Vicky is gone. "And do you hear that? It sounds like he's slamming himself into the door."

"Okay, but it's your job to keep an eye on him. I don't work all day to spend my nights cleaning up cat puke."

"None of us does," Amanda says, so quietly I'm not sure I really hear her, so maybe Danny doesn't. Or, maybe, he's letting this one go.

Amanda opens the door to let Buckles out, but he just stands there, looks up at her, and mewls. She sees the cut on his nose, smeary pinheads of cat blood on the back of the door. She starts to cry. There is vomit in the sink and in the bathtub. She scoops him up and cradles him, buries her face in his belly fur. She is sobbing and Buckles, declawed, is pawing at her hair.

I touch Amanda on the shoulder, then the back. How warm she is, beneath her dress, how feverish and soft. In a flash that passes so quickly it might not have happened, I imagine her kissing Uncle Danny, in their bed, with a woman's passion. Has he ever been able to equal her?

"Let me," I say, meaning clean up the vomit.

•　　　•　　　•

As I am getting into my car, Danny, who has walked me out, says, "Kyle." Even though he is the closest I have ever had to a father, there is always something formal in the way he says my name. His inflection is a horizon. It is a wall. He hands me some folded bills; I pocket them without looking. "So," he says, "I suppose we'll see you in a week."

Around the corner, idling at a stop sign, I see that Danny has given me two twenties and a ten, and I have to remind myself that my uncle has always been unselfish about money, from diapers to baseball gloves, and dinner once a week for how long? Things must be truly tight for Danny and Amanda now. I wonder if their situation is precarious enough to be undone by something like another vet bill and, if so, what that means if Amanda turns out to be not okay. It must be this, and not the vomit, that led to his decision. But why isn't he taking care of it himself? Either things are so bad at his office that he can't skip out for a long lunch, or else he wants to be able to tell his family he doesn't know what happened, and not be lying.

"Man, my uncle is one crazy motherfucker," I tell Tyler. We're having beers at McCarren's because Sara's working so they're on the house. "You won't believe what he's got me doing."

Sara's over at the taps, waiting for a Guinness to settle so she can finish the pour.

I tell him.

"Shit," he says. "You think you'll be able to?"

There are some old timers at the far end. Lifers, Sara calls them. Sometimes I laugh hard at this and other times it makes me afraid.

"Hey, business is business."

"So, what'd he give you?" Tyler asks.

"Four hundred," I say.

Sara fumbles the keys out of her purse and then sets about negotiating one, the wrong one, into the lock. She tries another and that one works.

"I could use another drink," she says. She only had a few before closing, and then one while she cleaned up. I say I'll have one too and she eyes me, deciding whether to start in on the question of if I need another. I don't, probably, no, I know I don't, but if she doesn't start in—she doesn't—I will have what I want, which is different from what I need: what a surprise. She gets the vodka out of the freezer and I go for glasses, find some coffee mugs first, decide that these are good enough. Sara cuts hers with some grapefruit juice and we clink but don't toast anything. We move to the living room, sit in the ambient glow from the kitchen.

"It's almost not enough anymore," she says, breaking the silence. Should I ask what "it" is? No, that's clear enough. She rattles the ice in her mug. "Typical," she says, meaning my not answering, so I say, "I have to kill my uncle's cat tomorrow."

Neither of us is saying what the other wants to hear.

•   •   •

The first time I saw Sara naked we were teenagers. She had small high breasts and I came in my pants when she rubbed against me. Sometimes when we are being cute with each other she reminds me of that, and I remind her that I got another hard-on a few minutes later, which she went to *town* on, I always say, laughing, and we both laugh, and I tell her she's still got it and she tells me to prove it to her and then I do. We date and we break up and date, and there have been others, for both of us, sometimes when there shouldn't have been, but as the years have moved our old friends away, married them off, or put them in their graves, our rediscoveries of each other have lasted longer and longer. Right now, finally, temporarily, again, we are everything to each other.

When I enter the bedroom she's on her side, facing away from the door, covers up under her armpit, and, as I can see from how she's breathing, still awake. I take off my shoes and slip my watch and wallet into them. I take my jeans off. I approach her side of the bed instead of my own. I take her hand and pull at her. She slides her legs from beneath the bedclothes, lets me stand her up and turn her toward me so we are face-to-face. She is wearing only an old pair of white underwear, faded from a thousand washings and thin. Her pubic hair presses against the fabric; it looks like a topographic map, perhaps a map of us, if we, this, could be less a thing than a place. I touch her speckled shoulders, graze my fingers down her fleshy upper arms, the light hairs of her forearms, the backs of her hands, until our fingers touch: tips to tips. I lean in to kiss her. We kiss.

• • •

I get to Danny's in the early afternoon, later than he said to come, but it was a rough morning. We went out to breakfast, didn't talk much, then Sara dropped me off at McCarren's so I could get my car.

"I'll call you," I said.

"No you won't," she said. "You'll just show up here."

I let myself into the house. Buckles is sprawled, asleep, on an arm chair, the cut on his nose scabbed over, taking in the full afternoon light that sets the fringes of his fur aglow, as if haloed already. He stirs when I take him up into my arms but does not try to get away. I hold him close, as I saw Amanda do, flip the push lock on the sliding glass door, and stand fixed a moment, appreciating the stillness of the yard, a ghost of breeze barely troubling the surface of the lake and the blue, blue pool. I step toward the edge of the water and kneel down, the stippled aggregate pressing into my knees through my jeans. I can feel the little red marks it is imprinting. I slide one hand as gently as I can around the cat's neck and start to strangle him at the same time that I plunge him under.

It takes maybe a minute. I hold him down another minute to be sure, and then I am sure. As a final act of either defiance or submission, he has pissed in my uncle Danny's pool. I watch the yellowish cloud dissipate, consider pulling the chlorine bobber over the spot, then think to myself, enough already.

• • •

I bring Buckles back inside and lay him down in the guest bathroom shower. I wonder if his being locked in here most of yesterday was even why he was so docile—poor, fucked animal; exhausted, ready. I decide I should check around for any final piles of vomit, to really do this right, and find one in the living room, which I clean up with a tissue and toss out in the kitchen garbage. When I'm done, I'll put the cat in there too, put in a fresh bag, and take the full one with me, bring it to the dump or something. I check the kitchen, the dining room, the hall. The door to Amanda and Danny's room is closed, but Vicky's is open.

I examine Vicky's windowsills and look under her bed. Nothing. I open her closet to see if she still has that tee shirt I got her. It's all black jeans and old kiddie clothes and a couple of fancy dresses, Christmas and wedding things. Probably she keeps her tee shirts in her bureau, but in the top drawer I find only socks and underwear, most of which is plain. But a few pieces are surprising, and I am glad the garments are all just stuffed in. If everything had been folded and neat she might notice that someone had been in here, though she probably would figure it was only her parents, spot-checking for weed.

There are a few lacy pieces, blacks and one red, not very risqué, really, just hard to imagine on Vicky. This thong with the leopard-print front, say, is almost unbearably cheesy, but if she were standing in front of a boy, as Sara stood in front of me last night, he would fall to his knees in worship—how could he not?—and maybe Vicky will not miss just a single pair, if it is a black lacy and not the leopard print, of which there is only the one. I bring them to my nose—of course they only smell clean—then put them in my pocket and shut the drawer, thinking it is time to finish cleaning up and get going.

I turn around and there's Amanda, standing in Vicky's doorway.

I guess she took the whole afternoon off work, came home after her appointment. I wonder what the results were, and how long she has been here. Was she here this whole time, maybe taking a nap? She has been watching me, silently, and is still silent, though she seems about to speak right now.

It is next Wednesday and my mother is saying, "Why aren't you over at Danny's?" and I'm telling her anything, or else I'm walking in to McCarren's, taking a seat at the far end, and Sara's ignoring me at first but then coming over, rolling her eyes, bringing a foaming beer for me, saying, "You're here early for a change," and I'm giving her that same old smile, the one that barely makes rent, the one that coasts into the station on fumes.

It is not next Wednesday. It is still this moment and that will be true of every moment that follows, assuming this moment ever ends, which, if I am lucky, it won't. Amanda filling the doorway, silent, us facing each other like friends or like family or like lovers: an eternity of silence and afternoon light. And she doesn't even know about the cat yet. I will never escape this town.

ESTRELLAS Y RASCACIELOS

The anarchists were drinking victory shots and making toasts because even though they'd never met with success before they surely knew it when they saw it or it found them. Snapcase, his beard effulgent with spilled drink, was sure that school was out for*ever.* He'd tossed Jessica's survey of art history, his own *Norton Shakespeare,* and somebody's copy of Derrida's *The Gift of Death* into the fire pit they had dug in the backyard. The shallow hole was surrounded by salvaged chairs and shaded by a blue canvas canopy they'd stolen from some resort because property was always already theft anyway, and plus they had really wanted that canopy. The books were doused with whiskey from a bottle of Ancient Age. Snapcase lit a hand-rolled cigarette and then tossed his still-burning match into the shallow pit. It went out in the air, so he lit another and placed it gingerly in a little pool of whiskey. It snuffed there. Someone said something about lighting three matches in a row. Somebody else said no, the expression was no three on a match. And how that expression had come from World War I, because if you lit three cigarettes off one match in your foxhole or trench the enemy in his foxhole or trench had three pins of light to triangulate your location and then he blew up everything or maybe just shot you and your two buddies.

Knock off the history book shit, Snapcase said. Where were the history books anyway? His fire was still unlit. The other anarchists who'd been watching were disappointed. I have to be at work in an hour, one said. Snapcase went back into the house for the history books. He ran into David in the living room.

But I like Nietzsche, David said, grabbing back his dog-eared copy of *The Antichrist,* which Snapcase had just taken from the bookshelf. Though no less certain in his convictions, David was not prepared to burn his *Dictionary of Critical Theory* and the books to which that book was a kind of skeleton key.

Yeah but if, Snapcase said.

Hey, why do you call yourself Snapcase? someone said.

Dude, someone else said, it's a *band.* Don't you know anything about hardcore?

David handed over his copy of *The Prophet Armed* because Trotsky had ordered the Russian anarchists shot down like partridges. Burn it, he said, and Snapcase went back outside. David eyed Estrella. She was finishing a rum and soda, going to pour herself some more rum, discovering there was no more rum, cursing. The label was ridged with silver like pirate booty. The Captain leaned on his sword. The TV was on. With the left rabbit ear twisted down so it touched the thick steel strings of their red electric bass, they were able to get one local station. Not having cable wasn't a statement. Maybe the statement was being made by the people who paid out a monthly portion of their slave wages for endless infomercials and Wolf Blitzer. Anyway it didn't matter because there was only one piece of news today. A single clip had been looping for hours. It was a bottle of light rum that was empty. Hakim Bey and *Pirate Utopias* notwithstanding, none of them had much stomach for dark.

Estrella was the loudest anarchist of them all. Her band had a song that went *We'll tear down fucking everything / Till stars are the reigning light / Estrellas y Rascacielos / Burning in the ungoverned night.* The bassist wrote the lyrics and she sang them. He loved it when she sang the line he wrote with her name in it. She loved singing her own name. The bassist always said he wrote the line in homage to the great Spanish anarchists, such as whoever. Actually it was because he loved her. When she sang her own name as part of his lyric it was like she had let him name her. She could sing so fucking loud. The band was a hardcore band. Her guitar roared like a certain kind of sermon. His bass rattled the windows and doors. The big gigs were coming soon; he just knew it. He was passed out under the kitchen table. The TV screen filled again.

David asked to see Estrella's new tattoo. She lifted her black hoodie from the waist. A circled *A* nested between her breasts, which were too small to hang but would have hung if they'd been bigger. Estrella knew that bras were just more bullshit, though sometimes she would put on a sports bra if she guessed they were probably going to be running away from something before their night was over.

I thought it would be cool to get it on my nipple, she said, but the guy said if I did that I might never be able to breastfeed.

What? David said.

Snapcase gathered dead leaves and put them into the pit and then lit those, and finally the books caught fire.

It's gonna rain, someone said.

It's gonna pour, someone else said, and that person was correct. It had been raining earlier but that had been a mere warm-up compared to what would come; that is, with what came.

I like it, David said to Estrella, but it's too bad.

He meant about her breasts, and not being able to get the nipples tattooed, or pierced even. He thought of the phrase *female troubles.* The silver ring centered in her lower lip gave her a pouty look, or rather accented the pout of her dark eyes and dark hair and the donned hood of the hoodie and the fact that she was frequently pouting. Her dreadlocks were wild and attractive. When she did push the hood back, as she had done, the dreadlocks made her seem more dangerous or unpredictable, but less severe. David wondered if her kiss had a metallic aftertaste, or if the salt and wet of her would overwhelm everything else.

They drank whiskey and watched the fire burn in the shallow pit until the downpour drowned the flames. Then everyone went back inside to watch the TV. Someone said for smokers to use the front porch and someone else said we should be able to smoke inside on account of the rain and the occasion.

We're out of rum and I don't want any more whiskey, Estrella said.

The liquor store was closing up when I bought the rum, David said.

This is only the first blow against the empire, someone said, and someone else said, Yeah but what a blow I mean boy you know?

There was a line at the gas station when I walked past it, David said. It went around the block. Everyone was filling their tanks and buying up the canned food. I walked in and stole two big bottles of Coke and nobody noticed.

It's on tape though, someone said. It's in the files. Someone else said that Coca-Cola had sponsored death squads in South America and that person was correct. Coca-Cola was also responsible for the following: environmental devastation in India, union-busting, wage-slavery, rotting the gums of children and adults, inventing the modern image of Santa Claus as part of a plot to commoditize Christmas (actually, the modern Santa Claus evolved from a series of Thomas Nast illustrations that appeared in *Harper's Weekly* between

1863 and 1865; the Coke Santa was done by the Swedish il-
lustrator Haddon Sundblom in the 1930s, long after the ar-
chetype was standardized), partnering with McDonald's,
sponsoring various execrable campaigns, here and abroad,
those death squads, and much more. So that person was really right for the most part when he or she said those things
about the soda they were all drinking but at least had stolen.

I bet that one store's open, Snapcase said, and we could
go get beer. But I don't want to go.

I'm really leaving now, said Roger, who sometimes went
by Dagger but couldn't commit to the alias. He fashioned a
rain hat from a plastic bag in which some Chinese food had
been delivered. He was the one who'd said earlier that he had
to go to work.

Lots of people were milling around, watching the TV and
deciding what they thought or already knowing or thinking
they already knew. Nobody knew Estrella's real name was
Anne. Even the ones who had been *with* her didn't know. She
was that good. Sometimes she almost forgot she had a real
name—she was *that* good. The rain beat harder on the windows. The shallow pit overflowed. David said he'd go to the
store and Estrella said she'd go with him. She went to look
for her boots. The anarchists pooled their money.

Angel, Snapcase, this guy they didn't really know but
who'd been crashing at their place, and Jessica were looking
out the back window at the fire pit. I guess it's a book *drown-
ing*, Angel said, and the guy they didn't really know mentioned Prospero and then someone put a Fifteen record on

and turned it up real loud. *Everybody knows authority is just abuse anyway / Everybody knows it ain't no use anyway / Kill your elected official today / We will win . . .* Estrella couldn't find her boots so David took his boots off in solidarity.

Muddy street dirt squished between David's toes. He told Estrella they needed to go faster, and she ran so far ahead that he almost lost her in the shifting sweeping curtains of water. The storm was a North Florida special. They hurtled through it like airplanes. The water in his eyes blurred his vision. She'd pulled her hood tight but her dreadlocks were soaked anyway. She stepped on a little shard of glass, landed badly, and twisted her ankle. David caught up to her.

Ow, she said, I mean fuck. She shut her eyes tight because it hurt and because she didn't realize that with all the water running down her face he couldn't tell she was crying so she was safe.

She shifted to her good foot and hopped. She landed, wobbled, steadied herself, hopped again. David slid a hand under her arm, his other behind her knees. He lifted her and carried her through the rain like a husband with a wife or a monster with a cherished victim. He carried her to the nearest house that had an overhang. The sudden freedom from the rain was cold and thrilling. He helped her sit, then knelt before her. He took her wounded foot into his hands. She was sitting in a puddle but there was nothing they could do about that. The whole world was a river that day, rising: taking and bringing things. He cleaned her foot as best he could in the puddle, wiping away the shiny trickle of blood that flowed from the cut on her sole. He suckled. The blood was metallic; his mouth did not even fill with it. It wasn't a bad cut, really.

I think it's out, she said. You didn't swallow it?

I don't know, he said. It was really small.

Is that okay? I mean will something happen to you?

I didn't think about that, he said.

His selflessness touched her. She considered what that might mean. This tender moment was ending but they'd always have it.

They stepped back out into the rain. Estrella hobbled, David walked. The day had been good and it was still cresting. They had shared a victory and lived by their principles, especially those of solidarity and mutual aid. The store was open. The beer was cold. There would be time later for regret and whatever the bassist thought, but right then they were still free. A pair of real anarchists, they drank on the street as they strolled home even though it was broad daylight and still raining.

THE NEW LIFE

I turned twelve on August 9, 1995, a few weeks before the start of the new school year and the same day that Jerry Garcia was dying in California, not that I knew it then. My parents had decided to have my party at the house, in our backyard: Slip 'n Slide, water balloons, the garden hose. I remember being worried it was too babyish but actually we had a pretty good time. Fun in the sun, you know? A real South Florida birthday. A Winn-Dixie sheet cake with a sports theme. I remember all of this so vividly, and can see myself living it, as if then-me is somebody else and now-me is a camera capturing him. Thirteen candles are lit (one to grow on) and I'm leaning in over the cake, waiting for the song to wrap up so I can blow them out. My best friend Kenny Beckstein and my dad are on either side of me, and the rest of the kids are clustered loosely around us, like apostles. My dad's smile is not forced, exactly, but you can see it's strained. He and Mom had been arguing about something earlier. Kenny's face is an altogether different story. He's got this look of pure adoration, ecstasy really, like he's never loved anything so much as he loves me right then.

I met Kenny in first grade. He was fat and I was a runt, a quick crier. We traded being last one picked for whatever the game of the day was, unless it was dodge ball, because I was so hard to hit. He and his big sister Angela were Irish twins—eleven months between them, and I was six months older than Kenny, so really it was like we were all the same age, but because of how the school calendar fell she was a grade ahead of us, and had gone off to the middle school last year. But now we would be middle schoolers too. Sixth grade.

But middle school wasn't good to Kenny, who still brought a dweeby plastic thermos of grape juice with his lunch instead of a soda can. He got knocked around in the locker room. Cheeks flushed, eyes glistening, relaxed-fit jeans held up out of reach in that jock asshole Zak Sargent's raised fist. Zak was in Angela's grade. He was a golden boy, a terrorist. I tried to teach Kenny to hold his own, but the truth was that what I knew how to do was be invisible, and this made me angry—at myself because it was all I could do, at Kenny because it was the one thing he couldn't. I lashed out at him, picked fights over anything stupid, said I was coming over and then didn't come. By winter break I'd stopped talking to him altogether.

I told myself that Kenny languished on the one rung of the social ladder I knew I was above, though in order to believe this I had to first accept the increasingly dubious premise that either of us was on that ladder at all.

In seventh grade an invitation came in the mail: his bar mitzvah. His parents must have forced him. I was lucky to have checked the mail myself that day, because if my parents had seen it they would surely have forced me.

Kenny spent the summer after eighth grade with his aunt and uncle. Their kids were a little older and they had a summer place way up in Maine.

I saw him on the first day of ninth grade—high school, the *real* big time—down the hall from me, in motion. He was taller, and not so zitty as he'd been. He was lean now, hair the color of wheat and shaggy about his ears. We saw each other, thirty feet of emptying hall between us. The bell was ringing—a digital bell that sounded like some bag of microwave popcorn was ready. The linoleum floors were freshly buffed for the new school year and the light flung down by the fluorescent tubes screamed back up at the ceiling. It was like being trapped between two horrible moons. He nodded at me—one acknowledging chin raise, that was all it was— and I gave him the same back. We were zeroed out, I understood this, strangers about to meet for the first time, though we didn't. Not then. We had classes to get to and were both late.

The same kids who had made middle school hell now greeted Kenny with elaborate high fives that climaxed with finger snaps. They sought him out. He was seldom by himself, in the hall or at lunch, but retained a sort of loose air of aloneness, which is not to say he ever looked lonely. He was standoffish and comfortable, genial but indifferent. He let the cool kids buy pot from him and court his interest in other ways. He had freedom of movement in and through every circle. He came and went. People called him Beck.

Angela, by this point, had been a goth for a couple of years. She had dyed her hair black and gotten her license at the end of September. She started driving her mother's old Volvo station wagon to school. Mrs. Beckstein drove a Saab now. I was old enough to go for my restricted license, but hadn't. Usually, I walked home. It only took like a half hour, and everyone knew the bus was for losers, but when it rained I had to scrub a ride, and one gray October day it came to pass. The two of them were standing there, together in the thickening drizzle, while Angela finished a clove cigarette. It smelled like musky candy.

"What up, Beck?" I said. I had never called him that before. The pert little word felt too smooth coming out of my mouth, like my tongue wanted to stumble, but on what? The word was a slick river stone. He'd been Kenny our whole lives. But this was his thing now, right? I could do it the new way. A fresh start. The nods. *Just be cool.*

"You still live six blocks from us?" Angela asked, and I couldn't tell if the question was a jab.

She popped in a Marilyn Manson tape. Excluding that noise, we rode back to our neighborhood in silence, which

Kenny finally broke by asking if I wanted to come over and smoke some pot.

The Beckstein house hadn't changed much. There was a new TV in the entertainment center, but the same old couch and lounger were side by side in front of it. I stood in the doorway and absentmindedly slipped my shoes off, assuming (rightly, as it turned out) that this was still house policy.

Angela turned back to look at me. I was just standing there, still in the doorway. I hadn't even shut the door.

"Come on," she said. "What's wrong with you?"

"Nothing," I said. "It's all good."

We went to Kenny's room. He led, then Angela, then me. I was hemming close to her, like a newborn doe to its mother, and accidentally mashed her heel. "Sorry," I said, and took a big step to one side. I felt like I was in a spotlight, on a stage. Kenny sat down on the gray-carpeted floor, leaning against his bed, and reached underneath, behind the dust ruffle. He pulled out a small green bubbler. He had his Oakleys pushed up onto the crown of his head like a tiara. He pulled the metal stem out of the bong and put his nose to the base. "I think this water's still good," he said, then sat it down by his knee while he broke up buds.

We sat with him on the floor.

A few bong loads made it around the circle, then Kenny reached under his bed again. This time he pulled out a shoe box. "Our cousin Jeff hooked me up when I was up there," he said, meaning Maine, presumably. This was the first conversation we'd had since 1995.

In the shoe box were concert bootlegs—cassette tapes. The Grateful Dead, the Disco Biscuits, the Dave Matthews Band, and worse things. Cousin Jeff, I learned, had taken Kenny to this two-day campout concert thing called Lemonwheel, thrown by a band called Phish at a decommissioned air force base near the Canadian border and named for a Ferris wheel they'd brought in for the occasion. The experience had apparently made a strong impression on Kenny. "Life-changing stuff, man," he said, and rummaged, picked out a Phish tape, crossed the room, and popped it in. He hit PLAY, didn't like what he heard, fast-forwarded to the end of the side, flipped it, and hit PLAY again. A guitar and piano were caterwauling. A cow bell went off like a dull shot. Something sounded like a vacuum cleaner.

After a while, Angela got up and left. It was impossible to tell how long, since the songs on the tape seemed to have no beginnings or ends, but rather melted into and out of each other. She said something I didn't quite catch that amounted, I think, to "Good to see you, Brad," and then she was closing Kenny's door behind her. A few seconds later I heard her bedroom door shut, followed by the twice-muffled rumble of Skinny Puppy or Jack Off Jill or NIN or more Manson— whatever it was she was into. And now we were alone with each other. Kenny had his eyes closed and was bopping his head, rhythmically, though not exactly in rhythm with the music. He was parallel to it, I thought, or maybe the rhythms related in some way I couldn't follow. I stared at him. Christ this was strong stuff, not like the dirt weed I'd been buying from a junior named Omar, stuff that made you giggly for a half hour then left you with nothing but a headache. The busy, winding music fragmented my thoughts, alienated my mind from itself. Things felt murky and televised. I couldn't help looking at Kenny—really drinking him in. He was stunning and I was seized with awe at the change he'd made, everything he'd sloughed off and become. I was still awkward, peripheral—the same as ever, save for the recent development of a downy mustache you could only see when the light was right. Jealousy washed over me, a sensation so powerful it was indistinct from either hatred or lust. The feeling lasted a deep stoned moment, which is to say I have no idea for how long. I felt choked, throat tight with need, mouth dry as if it had been swabbed out with a cloth. I wanted nothing but to cross that room and go to him.

I forced my gaze to the window. A dumb little grapefruit tree, the neighbor's hedge, a blue recycling bin. Cars in driveways. Yes, anything normal. His bedroom walls were the same, sponge-painted pale blue over an eggshell base, but the old outer space–themed border was gone. There were music posters now: Bob Marley with his head thrown back, laughing; a garish *Steal Your Face* on black light felt; a full-page photo of the guys from Phish had been torn from a recent issue of *Rolling Stone* and taped to the wall by his desk. But wherever I looked, my eyes invariably wound up on him again: quickly away, long circle back. His eyes were closed. He was in deep space. I was fidgeting, making adjustments to hide a formidable erection.

"Totally bitchin', isn't it?" Kenny said, thankfully without opening his eyes. He meant about the stupid music, or maybe the quality of the drugs.

"Yeah dude," I said. "For real."

Angela would tear out of the school parking lot, wheels squealing because why? Because fuck *you*, is why, she'd have said if anyone had asked her. But who would ask? I loved the sound of the old family car yowling like an agitated cat. We'd pick up drive-thru burgers or Taco Bell, head back to their place, and get ripped. Her fat friend, Dawn, another goth, drove a black Suburban. She'd follow us back to the neighborhood, drop her car off at her house, then walk over.

Dawn was loud. She caked her face in some powder that couldn't hide the craters in her cheeks; instead it cast them in white relief. Her eyeliner, black, ran in the heat. She believed she was making progress in the study of witchcraft and was objectionable on more or less every level. Angela said she believed in Dawn, that the fat girl *did* know magic. They would hang out with us as long as Kenny didn't put his music on, which he inevitably did, because he hated Dawn fiercely. Indeed, she was one of the few subjects he allowed to trouble his easy-does-it-no-sweat veneer, I think because she reminded him of his old self. She had never learned to molt, and seeing her in the sweaty cage of her body unearthed the worst of what he had struggled to bury.

Kenny and I never talked about—even mentioned—the old days. I knew that to do so would be to betray him all over again. It was a shame, though, because Angela was attached to Dawn, and I was hard-fallen for Angela, and I think on some level Kenny knew this, and in our whole lives he was never anything but kind to me. He would hold out on the music for as long as he could stand to.

It doesn't get cold in South Florida until after New Year's, and it doesn't even get that cold. No scarves and gloves. A few weeks of sweater weather is about it. But November? Forget it. You could go swimming. *We should go swimming,* I thought. I was standing in the Beckstein kitchen, stoned to the gills, pouring myself a glass of orange juice.

"That's stupid," Dawn said.

"I don't know," Angela said. "Sounds kinda nice. Swimming high. Like the womb or something."

"I don't have a suit," Dawn said.

"Go home and grab one," Angela said. "We'll wait for you, or if you want I can come with."

Dawn gave her friend what was clearly intended to be a withering look, but Angela didn't. This was to all of our surprise, including, I think, Angela's. She said, "Well, I'm going to go change."

Kenny loaned me a pair of shorts. I put them on in the guest bathroom, then helped him move the stereo out back. Dawn was sitting upright on one of the lounge chairs, smoking a clove. She hadn't even taken her shoes off. She was already sweating.

"Not even gonna dip your toes?" I asked.

"Better not put on any of that hippie shit," she replied.

"I'm sorry," I said to her, "do you live here?"

"Neither of us lives here," Dawn said to me.

"Hey Dawn," Kenny said, "why don't you shut the fat fuck up?"

Angela came out of the house. She was wearing a black bikini with string ties that rode low on her notchy hips. Her legs were a bone-white mile. There were freckles on her chest and face, a mole on her left shoulder. She seemed to catch fire as she stepped out from under the overhang and into the undiminished autumn sun. Her toenails, I saw, matched her fingernails, and both matched the bikini. *Okay,* I remember thinking, *I'll just be in love with them both then.*

Kenny lazed in the shallow end, floating on his back. Dawn lit another clove off the butt of the old one and sulked, watching her friend do laps. She didn't want to be there, but it was a long time before she left.

Over winter break, Angela tore her Nine Inch Nails posters off her walls. Her fishnets, her black boots, her goth makeup—all down the memory hole. When we went back to school, she was in blue jeans with plain tee shirts and looked like she belonged in a public service announcement.

Kenny's birthday was in February. He was fifteen too, finally. I didn't know what to get him. He only liked two things, and there was no sense trying to find a better pot connection than the one he already had, so I went to the record store. He had nearly a hundred tapes by this point, but a lot of them were incomplete or fuzzy recordings, and he—a late-comer but a purist—owned almost nothing on CD. There wasn't a lot of Phish to choose from, except for one double live album I knew he already had, but there was a ton of Grateful Dead stuff. Studio albums, "official bootlegs," best-of comps. Then I saw it: 2/11/69 at the Fillmore East in New York City. They'd been opening for Janis at the time, and this package had two discs marked EARLY SHOW and LATE SHOW. The eleventh was his birthday. I wasn't sure if he would already have the show on bootleg, but if nothing else it'd be a sound quality upgrade from the tape version. I bought it, took it home, thought about wrapping it, didn't, switched it from the clear plastic bag it had come in to a brown paper one, pulled it back out of the brown bag, dug around in the kitchen junk drawer, found a Sharpie. I pulled the shrink wrap off so I could write directly on the case. *Fifteen years later & there you were,* I wrote, and put the thing back in the brown bag.

On the day itself, Mrs. Beckstein picked him up from school an hour early to go take the test for his restricted license. I waited at the house with Angela. We were on the living room couch, side by side, staring at the TV, unaccustomed to afternoon sobriety. She was flipping channels, paused briefly on MTV, a video for some angry song the old her would have cherished. "Stupid," she said, to herself I was pretty sure, then went back to flipping—CSPAN, Jesus station, Spanish Jesus station, Home Shopping.

"Can I ask you a question?"

"Huh?" she said.

"Can I ask you a question?"

"No, I mean what's the question?"

"Well, you've like, changed."

"That's not a question."

"Yeah, I guess not."

"I don't really know how to explain it," she said. "It feels a lot like traveling. Movement. Some urge like birds get."

"Whales. They go far, right?"

"I don't know, maybe, yeah. I like birds better. I want a tattoo of a bird. Something that flies over the ocean."

"Don't get a seagull," I said. "They're scavengers. They smell."

"Something else then."

Her lips were dry and not as soft as I'd imagined. She exhaled through her nose, a tickle skittering across my face. "Don't do that again," she said. "They'll be back any minute." And they were.

Kenny had passed the test. He had his learner's permit. I congratulated him, then gave him his CD. "Hey cool," he said. "Let's go throw it on." I knew the songs now, some by their opening riffs and others not until I heard the lyrics, but I got there, usually. Kenny told me the names of the ones I'd never heard.

I was in the cafeteria, sitting by myself because lunchtime was when Kenny did most of his dealing. It was the end of March. I had forgotten my lunch that morning, and was eyeing the line, trying to decide if it was worth getting involved in. Dawn plopped herself down next to me. She smelled like sour sweat and old smoke. She tented her meaty fingers. "We're losing her," she said.

"Who's 'we'?"

"The fact that you didn't ask 'who's her' just proves how right I am."

"So Angela Beckstein's too cool for us lately. What do you want from me?"

"I have a ritual—"

"Oh Christ, here we go—"

"But I can't do it by myself."

"Aren't you a little old for playing pretend?"

"It'll bring her back to us."

But what was there, really, to bring Angela back from? She was a person who had made a decision, a change, probably for the positive—at least if measured by any standard other than our warped own. I'm sure her parents, for example, were sleeping better than they had in years.

Here's what Dawn couldn't stand: Angela was dating Zak Sargent, who had grown into exactly the kind of cartoon character his name suggested. He'd become what we'd all always known he would. And Zak was a whole package. New friends, a suite of attitudes and hangout spots—the new life Angela had told me she was looking for. She was out over the ocean now.

I hated Zak Sargent, too. I hated what he represented,

and I hated him for everything he'd ever done to Kenny, so much of which I'd witnessed or turned my face away from, and of course because now he had Angela. Zak Sargent would spend most of his life having and doing and getting whatever he wanted. I knew that. It was a great sick truth. Zak Sargent had led the pogroms of childhood, and since me and Kenny were best friends again, I lived every day with the knowledge that I would have joined those raiding parties if they'd only been willing to include me. But they hadn't, and with nothing on which to base a claim for some portion of guilt, how could I ever hope to be forgiven?

She got to my house at ten till midnight. I met her in the side yard and led her around back. She was wearing black jeans and a long-sleeved black shirt with silver buttons. It was tight on her. She had a small blue backpack slung over her shoulder.

"So where did you learn about this spell?" I asked.

"Oh, I'm past learning other people's spells," she said. "This is my own thing."

The moon was three-quarters full. We walked past the picnic table and out of the bright perimeter established by the outside security lights. We stood near the back fence, in a pool of shadow cast by our lone oak. Bugs buzzed and whizzed. She started taking things out of the bag: a coffee mug with the cast of *The Muppet Show* on it, a pair of black fishnet stockings, a votive candle in a little glass, a fillet knife, a can of shaving cream. The fillet knife had a wooden handle on which she'd drawn upside-down crosses and devil stars.

She pointed to the knife and mug. "These are our chalice and blade."

"What about the stockings?"

"Our personal item. They're a locus of essence. It's how we target the spell."

"You mean they're Angela's?"

"Yeah, obviously. What would a pair of my stockings do?"

"Where did you get them?"

"She left them over at my house one time."

"And you never gave them back?"

"Does any of this matter?"

"You're just sick is all."

"Eat a dick, Brad."

She drew a circle of power in the grass with the shaving cream.

"This way when we're done you can clean it up," she said. "It was this or spray paint, but we needed something."

"Good choice," I said. I had no idea how to be nice to her.

She knelt down in the circle, chanted a while in Latin, then motioned for me to join her. I knelt, too. We were facing each other, close enough to touch but not touching. She took a book of matches from her pocket and chanted—a rushed low garble with lots of edges—while she lit the votive. A fake ripe blueberry smell.

"We're lucky there's not much wind tonight," she said, then checked her watch. "Three minutes till. It's time."

She unbuttoned her cuffs, rolled them up to her elbows, then instructed me to tie Angela's stockings around her wrists. I tied her up loosely, one leg to each wrist, so the empty waist swung low between her arms and brushed the grass. She had full freedom of movement, and took the mug-chalice from my hands. "Pick up the knife," she said. I did. "Okay," she said, and unbuttoned the top three buttons of her shirt. She pulled the fabric back, and drew a short horizontal line with her finger across the flat space below her clavicles but above the tops of her breasts. "Not too deep," she said, "but not too shallow either. I only want to have to do this once."

"I don't understand," I said.

"Nothing's free in this world, Brad," she said, "or in the other. You pay for what you take."

We were in love with the same girl and neither of us was ever going to have her. I had come to terms with this. But here was Dawn, fat horrible Dawn, alive with her yearning, ready to face down the very universe on behalf of her unanswerable desire.

"I want to be the one," I said.

"No, this part isn't for you. It's mine."

"I'm not cutting you," I said. I reached for her wrists. She pulled back but I grabbed the stockings by their crotch. *Angela,* I thought, and tugged so Dawn pitched forward, her face close enough to mine for kissing. I needed that scar for myself. "Do it to me or it doesn't happen. It's less than a minute to midnight. You're out of time."

I pulled my tee shirt off and tossed it outside the power circle.

She took the knife back and proffered the coffee mug, which I took by the handle. "No," she said, "hold the bottom, with both hands, like you would with any other chalice."

"Right," I said. "Any other chalice. Got it." She untied the stockings from her wrists and bound mine with them. Her movements were brusque and furious. She bound me tighter than I had her.

"Keep the chalice upright, keep the wound over the chalice, and try to catch more blood than you spill. I should have known you would ruin this for me."

I closed my eyes, thinking that there would be more chanting first, but it turned out that the time for talk had truly passed. There was nothing but the smell of grass, night's incidental music of bugs and dogs and distant cars, and Dawn's breathing, which I realized I suddenly no longer heard. She was holding her breath, we both were, and a knife doesn't make any noise at all, gliding over—through—your skin. Not even a *whish*. The sensation was of something slick and delicate, powerful yet deft, an ice skater perhaps. A swimmer. Then my vision seemed to prism, and the world became pain. I cried out—no, that wasn't my voice, it was Dawn's—and my eyes flew open and we saw each other and past her I could see lights coming on in my house. She had flinched, or if she hadn't I had, and the cut was too high up, life was pouring out of me in drafts, and no sound escaped my lips but one like air leaking out of a bike tire. I still had both hands on the chalice. I raised it up to my neck, and could feel it gaining weight in my hands. It was filling—quickly. I let it drop, heard it *thunk* in the grass.

I tasted blood, felt it boil out of my mouth, up over my lip, and down my chin. Dawn tried to stand, her legs buckled, then she got hold of herself and half-stumbled out of the power circle. Running would make things worse for her. They'd find her and there would be so many questions with no right answers. I knew a feeling of bright lift, even as my body sank to the ground. I was a balloon within myself, tethered by a skinny, frayed cord. Ear to the earth, I could hear feet thundering closer—my parents, no doubt—and realized that the witch had been right about everything, and I was glad to have helped her, though we had screwed the thing up so badly. Come to think of it, however, I didn't know enough about this stuff to declare our failure with any certainty. And if we *had* succeeded? What would there be for Angela to come back to? I hated to think we might have made things worse for her—we loved her, after all—and I concentrated my attention away from what was happening—it wasn't hard—I was only being shaken, and Mom was screaming—to puzzle out the question, but someone far away was slipping the soft bonds from my wrists and this action unstrung the tether as well. In the midst of absolving brightness I saw the beautiful answer and it was Kenny. The brother and sister would always have each other.

TENNESSEE

Off to the land of club soda unbridled

—David Berman, "Tennessee"

My little brother Rusty was on the back porch, lighting up.

"Hey," he said.

"Rusty," I said. "The smoking."

"This is what Mom and Dad made you come home for? To try some weird bonding shit against my smoking?"

"They didn't *make* me come home. It was a choice. I wanted to come."

"Ran out of money, you mean."

"What's with the smoking?"

"Do you know how many Jews there are at my high school?" Rusty said.

What happened is the family moved because my father lost a job and my mother got one. They left Miami, where we had always lived, and came to this suburb of Nashville. I think they picked it because it had the good school system for my brother, who hates his full name, Russell, and so goes by Russ in all circles except the family, where he has always been and will always be Rusty. Everyone agrees the move was hardest on him—especially him. Me, I say what's one suburb to another? We didn't actually live *in* Miami. Not like South Beach, Calle Ocho, and everything. We lived in a middle-class suburb called North Miami Beach, in the shadow of a wealthier suburb called Aventura, with the real city somewhere maybe half an hour south. These places were all part of the "greater Miami area," which was understood to be among the biggest Jewish communities in the country. Fourth biggest, people always said, though I don't know where they came by that number or who was in the top three. I was ten years old before I made a non-Jewish friend. (Her name was Marie Hahna and I fell right in love.)

"How many Jews are there at your high school?" I asked my brother.

"Eleven," he said. "And three of them are done after this year."

"Wow."

"You know what I heard one kid say to another?"

"What?"

"Three down, eight to go." Rusty smiled, a pleasureless near-grimace. He drew smoke and then blew it out slowly. It hung close about him like a morning mist.

"Oh come on, they didn't."

"Did."

"And this is a reason to smoke?"

Rusty's more right than he knows, about why I'm home. Or maybe he knows exactly how right he is and I'm the one who doesn't know.

When I called to ask for a little helping hand my father wouldn't even get on the phone, though I could hear him in the background. Boy, could I ever. Shouting and shouting. My mother, though no less disapproving, fostered a sort of muted respect for the time I had spent—in her words— *finding myself.*

She sent the money. Here I am.

In Miami, where everyone was a Jew, you didn't think about it. It didn't matter. It was assumed. You put in your time: Rosh Hashanah, Yom Kippur. Drone along with the congregation, slur the memorized phonetic Hebrew. Hello, Mrs. Nussbaum—*mazel tov* about your daughter. Forget black hats, wigs, holes in the sheet. We were Hannukah-and-lox Jews, not the Kashrut-and-Shabbos kind. But now we lived in a city with a mere four thousand Jews and a paltry three synagogues (my mother's figures). So my parents were finding *themselves,* making cultural overtures, like enrolling my brother in Youth Group and buying the *Schindler's List* deluxe box with the director's cut and survivor interviews.

Through some program at their new synagogue they had donated a small but not miserly sum to aid Jewish "settlers" in Israel, a designation I took strong issue with. Soon enough my father and I were standing on opposite sides of the kitchen table, on the edge of a blowout over Palestine.

"That bastard," my father said. "The one you read. That Chomsky, that—Jew-hating bastard!"

"Chomsky's Jewish," I said.

"A self-hating Jew, maybe," he said. "Like you."

"Hey," I said. "I don't hate myself, or the Jews. Now, what the Israeli government does on the other hand . . . I don't see how hating that or them has anything to do with Elijah, the fifth commandment, or us."

"Have you read the Dershowitz editorial I forwarded you? It explains everything. Everything."

The kitchen window looked out on the deck and there was Rusty, his back to the house, smoking. His friend Dara was there, too, facing us, maybe even watching us through the window? I wondered if she could she hear the fight. Dara was the prized only child of someone important at the synagogue. Her roots went back to its founding in 1843. My parents viewed the friendship as a profitable one. I wondered if she thought I was winning the argument.

"Dershowitz," I said. "Now there's a right-wing SOB I want to listen to. He's pro-*torture*, for the love of—"

"He's Jewish, at least," said my father. "You should hear the voice of your own people sometime. Might wake you up."

"CHOMSKY IS JEWISH!" I said. "Remember 'self-hating'?"

"Stop this," my mother said. We paused. "You two are here all day while your brother is at school and I'm working, and my parents are coming in at one o'clock on Wednesday."

We greeted this information with silence, my father especially.

"Therefore," she continued, "one of you will have to pick them up. Or you can both go. To be honest, I don't care. Just get them here."

My father was increasingly home-bound, so much so it made us uncomfortable, which is not to say that he didn't keep busy. He wrote letters to the editors—all of them—about Israel and Palestine. He cleaned the house.

Actually, the cleaning had become sort of worrisome, too. It was so thorough, almost as if he were trying to say that if he could no longer work in an office then by God he would keep such a spotless and ordered home that the family would come to see how his lost job had been a good fortune in disguise.

If you ask me, the worst part for Dad about my brother smoking was not the ruination of his young body or the ongoing disrespect of his doing it, but the white flecks of ash that clung to Rusty's clothes. That, and having to constantly change the air fresheners. There was a plug-in plugged in to every spare outlet in our house. He had even unplugged some lamps.

Like Jews raising swine on elevated platforms in the Holy Land, Rusty obeyed the letter of his father's law. He never smoked in the house. But Dad was convinced that the smell clung to his clothes, that he left bits of odor and ash everywhere he sat, soiling the couch fabric, the cushions on the kitchen chairs, everything. He may even have been right, in fact he probably was, but that wasn't the issue anymore. The house stank, not with cigarette smoke but with synthetic bouquets of every variety. It was potpourri without end, amen, and we all lived in its invisible, cloying crush.

My father decided he would cook a genuine Jewish brisket for the in-laws' first Tennessee meal. They were coming up from West Palm Beach and he thought the brisket would make for the perfect pastiche of Jewish and Southern tradition, to the extent that either could be embodied in a slab of beef.

Between that and cleaning the house, his day was full. So there I was, cruising down I-65 at the wheel of the family Volvo.

I was like a kid again, all nerves, afraid even to change the radio station until I was off the highway and stopped at a light. I hit a preset and the country music was swapped out for some guy who must have written his senior college thesis on Green Day, croon-yelling about a girl who had done everything wrong, and how broken up and drunk he was because of it. *It's no wonder Rusty's miserable. This mopey stuff just crushes your soul and—*

I realized that my opinion of the latest rock music was

sounding suspiciously like my father's old attacks on what I'd listened to at Rusty's age. This creeped me out. But I was getting off track. The goal was to bond with my brother, not critique his taste. If I could remember how the chorus went I could bring the song up later in a conversation. Maybe that would be a cool thing we could talk about. I started to sing along, willing the words to stick.

As the song faded out I registered a chorus of car horns. The light had changed and I had missed it. I hit the gas too hard and almost plowed into the guy in front of me. But didn't. I was getting the hang of things all over again.

At the next light I chanced a look into the glove box and sure enough there was a stray cigarette buried under the registration. Do I know my brother or what? I punched in the car lighter, one eye on the traffic light, killed the AC, and lowered the windows. The smells of cut grass and motor oil poured in, along with a lot more sunlight than I had counted on. You sit behind tinted windows for a while and you forget what the day is. I scanned the horizon. It was luscious country, all rises and slopes and green, with a few half-finished planned communities and strip malls, but still. It was mild, as blight goes—enough to make you worry for the future, but somehow not enough to wreck such a sweet summer day. I gawked at every horse in every pasture. The lighter popped back out and I touched it to the cigarette, thinking maybe this was the way into Rusty's head. I took a drag, started coughing. My eyes watered. The light changed. The horns started in again.

"Oh my, that smell," my grandmother said, pulling away from my hug. "What have you been doing—smoking?"

How do you explain this kind of thing to a grandma?

"You know, during the war," my grandfather said, "I was quite the smoker. Of course we didn't know then what we know now. Modern medicine and so forth."

"Don't tell me," I said, "tell Rusty. He's the one who needs to know."

"It's so *green* out here," my grandmother said. We were cruising. "And the hills are just—"

"I know," I said. "Don't you love it?"

"Prime real estate," my grandfather said knowingly. Before retirement he had headed some firm. Their golden years were shaping up just right.

"So how is everything?" my grandmother asked. "It's been so long."

"It's been okay," I said. "But you're pretty up to date. I mean, you talk to Mom twice a week, and I'm assuming you read my letters."

"I read them," my grandfather said. "She won't go near a computer. 'That machine,' she calls it. Like it's dirty! But I read her your letters."

"Sometimes he reads me your letters," my grandmother said. "But I won't go near that machine."

Sooner or later they would offer to buy me a suit. For job interviews. They would not ask me about my time away.

They were good people, good grandparents, but had their prerogative for sure.

Maybe you think my father didn't want to pick up his in-laws because he didn't like them. Oh they had their differences, sure. Jewish mothers, in-laws, all the clichés you can imagine just roiling together, lolling to the surface like matzo balls in soup. But I think it's that having my mother's parents around drives home how he doesn't talk to his own father anymore. I don't know what they fell out about, but they don't speak. My other grandpa is eighty-something. When I think of it, I call him. He sounds far away and confused, down in Florida near Dad's sister and the place we left. Grandpa and Dad didn't even say good-bye.

Rusty was upstairs, in his room. I let myself in. "They're here," I said.

"Don't ever come in here without knocking," he said.

"Did you ever even ask any of your friends if you could stay with them?" I said. "You didn't, did you? The Weissbergs have got the room. They'd have taken you. We've known them how long?"

"What would have been the point of asking?" he said. "Dad kept going on about breaking up the family. 'What with your brother off and gone already,' he kept saying. If I had asked the Weissbergs it would have been worse. Because they would have said okay and Dad would have wanted to say okay, but he wouldn't have been able to, or he'd have said okay and then had to take it back. Either way it'd have killed him."

"How can you know that?" I said.

"How can you not know that?" he said.

And he was right, was the thing. My little brother, Rusty, with his restricted driver's license and his smoker's cough, had it pegged. It would have gone just like that—him screaming "I'll never" with all the teen angst he could muster, which was plenty. And he would have lost. Our father could be the most stubborn and solipsistic of God's creatures, even if it left him lonely as a goat. The isolation was a kind of fuel, I think. And though the two of them were in that regard nearly identical, in the end it wouldn't have been a battle of wills. It had been a question not of wanting but of suffering, and the still-deeper truth of the matter was that it had not been a question at all. And so now, maybe, Rusty was going to smoke himself to death just to spite them.

Dara dropped by. My mother introduced her parents. My grandmother invited her to stay for dinner. My father groaned. My mother turned and gave him a look.

"What?" she said. "There's plenty."

It wasn't that he had anything against Dara. To the contrary, he thought she was a very good influence—I'd heard him say so in just those words (not like Rusty's layabout bum of a big brother, seemed to be the implication). It was the presumption he objected to, his in-laws inviting somebody to dinner in *his* house!

Dara, smart girl, went off to find Rusty, who was out on the back deck again.

"It's good that Rusty has such a nice little friend," my grandmother said to me.

"His little friend is not so little," my grandfather said. I couldn't help but laugh. It was true. Dara was seventeen, a looker even though she dressed down. Or maybe that was just when she came over to our house. I tried to imagine what she'd look like primed for a night on the town. The kids, I had been told, made a popular hangout of the Sonic Burger down Hillsborough Road, where they'd all meet up after the school football games.

Okay, so maybe *some* things were different from Miami.

"Does Rusty date that girl?" my grandmother asked.

"No," my mother said. "Or—well I don't know exactly, but don't bring it up with him, okay?"

"If Rusty doesn't date that nice girl," my grandmother said, turning to me, "then you should ask her on a date."

"Grandma, she's like a kid."

"I was engaged to be married at her age," my grandmother said. "And by the time I was your age I had already given birth to your uncle Steve." My father shook his head. His brother-in-law's wife is a crazy goy bitch and we don't talk to either of them anymore.

"It was a different world," my mother said to her mother.

"A nice Jewish girl comes to a house with two eligible young men and can't get herself so much as asked on a date."

"Daniel doesn't need to date his brother's friends," my mother said, "and Rusty's life is complicated enough as it is."

"Why is his life so complicated, I want to know?" my father interjected. "He goes to school, he has his friend, he smokes those damn cigarettes just to make me crazy. He doesn't even get all A's. His life is cake and pie."

"He got one B," my mother said, "and it was in phys ed."

"Those damn cigarettes—" my father said. Mom just shook her head.

My father was in high school when his parents moved him from some Long Island suburb of no particular distinction to a sunnier, if equally indistinct, suburb of Miami. He should have been glad to escape the fate of that life, but you know how it is—his friends, the places he knew, a girl probably, all his baseball cards. He lost everything, and swore to himself to hate the new state, city, school, life. But couldn't. He loved South Florida, almost right off the bat. He met my mother there, started his family, and was even heard to say that it was where he expected to die. But none of that love and happiness enabled him to forgive his own parents for the trauma that made it all possible. Whatever he finally fell out with my grandfather over, I know it was really over this.

One thing my father always swore: he would never do to his children what his parents did to him. But then God, who they say works in His own ways and who can be so cruel, made it so the trauma had to be passed down like a rite of passage. Whether or not Rusty ever forgives him, our father will never forgive himself. Nobody ever tried harder than that man, but some things are just beyond control, like if Abraham had had to go through with the sacrifice of Isaac, but somehow Isaac lived, and then when it was time God made Isaac put the knife to Jacob.

Even my mother's parents know to withhold comment on the thick air-freshener atmosphere, that fake-clean floral stench, that reek of grasping for control. They kvetch about everything, but never that.

Smells are the easiest to get used to anyway. After a few minutes you hardly even notice. If you're out of the house for a while, okay, it hits pretty hard when you come back in. But you just wait.

"What a place Germany was," my grandfather said, gesturing with his fork—not so much stabbing as nudging the space in front of him.

"You're flicking brisket juice," my grandmother scolded. He put the fork down.

Grandpa favored baby blue golf shirts and ran his left hand over his bald, liver-spotted head when he was feeling wistful. "Such culture," he said. "And even with the war on there was plenty of time. I used to know quite a bit of the native tongue. Very much like Yiddish, German. I couldn't read Goethe, maybe, but who wants to read Goethe? I could order dinner, I could ask directions. What else could I have wanted?"

"To read Nietzsche?" I said. "Or listen to Mozart in the original?" My grandfather loves opera so I figured I could force an ally out of him.

"Jew-hating bastards—the both of them," my grandmother said. Her thing was heavy necklaces and doing her hair up with spray. It was retirement condo chic and they had taken to it as well as other kinds of Jews took to yarmulkes, black coats.

"How would you know?" I asked.

"I know what I know," she said.

"He's like this," my father said. "Always siding with the Jew-haters."

"Dara," my mother cut in, "are you looking forward to the new school year?"

"I'm going to spend a quarter in Israel," Dara said. All the grown-ups at the table went *ooh*.

"It's very lovely there," my grandmother said. "We've been a number of times."

"You're going to learn so much," my father said.

"Very modern," my grandfather said. "All the amenities. Not like some of the places we've been to." He glared, half-kidding half-serious, at his wife. She liked to travel to exotic places on senior discount tours. When they would get back, Grandpa would start his recollection of the trip by saying, *Now, when I was a soldier fighting Hitler in the Second World War, I thought the living was rough, but let me tell you . . .*

"Israel," I said. It was too easy, it was totally pointless, and I was going to do it anyway. "Try not to get blown up by an insurgent."

"THEY'RE NOT INSURGENTS THEY'RE FA-
NATICS!" my father said.

"They can be both," I said.

"MURDERERS," my father said.

"They can even be all three," I said.

"Please," my mother said.

"Okay," Rusty said. "We're leaving the table now."

"You may be excused," my mother said.

"It wasn't a question," Rusty said.

"Thanks for dinner, Mr. and Mrs. Kessler," Dara said.

"What a shame," my grandfather said. "A boy who can't
respect his own heritage."

"I'm twenty-three," I said.

"And after everything you fought for," my father said.
"In the war."

"The things I saw," my grandfather said. "Things I
couldn't even tell you."

I happen to know that my grandfather never saw any combat,
or liberated any camps. He was part of a company that mostly
ran supplies from one base to another. The only time he even
fired his service rifle was when he happened upon a poor, war-
burdened peasant family in some rural area and took down
a deer with one perfect shot. And the peasant family was so
thankful and had plenty to eat and hugged him and wished
him good luck and he never had to fire the gun again.

Come to think of it, that might have been my other grandfather's story. They were both enlisted men. But how hard is

that to picture? These crabby old Jews with their hiked-up pants and endless kvetching. And one of them I haven't laid eyes on in how many years? These guys, I'm supposed to believe, won a war.

I'm not a bad son. Only prodigal. I know they fought and served, I just can't picture it. You know? My dad, now him I can picture—I've seen the pictures. Vietnam? Student defer-ment. Like a good Jewish boy? Yeah, with the hair down to his ass and the leather vest. Like you wouldn't believe. Imag-ine what his mother, the Polish immigrant, must have said.

It got late. The parents and grandparents went to bed. So, I decided, what better time to bond with the brother? I knocked on his bedroom door. Turned out Dara was still hanging around. Well, what the heck? Bond with her, too.

I filched a bottle of scotch from my parents' liquor cabi-net and brought it upstairs, but they turned up their noses, so I brought them down to help choose. Vodka they were happy with. Don't ask me why. "Maybe it's the Russian blood," I said, as we walked with our fixed drinks out of the kitchen, through the living room, out to the deck.

"Huh?" Rusty said.

"The Russian in us. On Dad's side. Grandpa was born in Odessa, I think. Or his parents were. Somebody came over." We raised our glasses and drank. Rusty lit a cigarette.

·　　　·　　　·

It got really late. The deck chairs were dusted with that gray-ish outdoorsy shmutz they get, so we were sitting on the deck itself, our backs against the quiet house. We stared into that country darkness. Rusty kept stubbing his smokes out on the deck; really grinding them in. One after another after an-other. I kept waiting for the drinks to loosen him enough that he'd spill his guts, his secret hopes, something I could bond with, but he only looked off into the night or down at the pile of butts, which he'd arranged in a tiny pyramid.

"That's, uh, pretty cool," I said.

"That's gross," Dara said.

"You know what?" Rusty said. "I'm going to bed."

"I love you—bro," I said.

"Yeah, well." My brother went inside. Christ, he could be a pill sometimes. I thought it was damn decent of Dara to wait a few courtesy minutes before taking her leave. We shared a little silence, during which I turned the words "good Southern breeding" over and over in my mind, as if they were a little gem I was inspecting. But then I noticed that she still didn't seem to be going anywhere. And had she slid closer?

"So it's, uh, pretty cool that you're still here, uh, hanging out with me," I said.

"I don't want to die a virgin," Dara said, eyes on her drink.

Ahh shit, I thought. *Loosened the wrong one.*

"Like if I did get blown up on a bus or something. I'd have never even known what it was like."

"You're a virgin?"

"Does that surprise you?"

I didn't have an answer to that question.

"What about my brother?" I asked.

"Oh come on, he's like my best friend," she said. That had actually been my point. If you can't sublimate your fear of mortality into sex with your best friend, what's it there for?

"And there's no *other* guy at your school?" I said.

"Lose it to a goy?" she said, almost too bewildered by the suggestion to be dismayed by the prospect. Another silence ensued.

"You're not going to get killed in a terrorist bombing," I said, finally.

"You don't have to bullshit me," she said. "I know what you think of Israel."

"That a fact?"

"Russ told me how you hate their government."

"Well, to be fair," I said. "I hate every government, I guess, but why hate, say, the French government? I don't even know any French. I hate the government of the United States because it's mine, and so I can. And I hate the government of Israel because I'm a Jew, so I can do that too. Hating the government is every citizen's duty."

"You don't hate them because they deserve it?" she asked.

"Oh, they deserve it," I said. "But that's sort of not even the point."

●　　　●　　　●

The syrupy cloy was fresh all over again when we stepped inside, and lightly sickened my drunk. I took a deep breath and held it; the air filled my lungs and burned there. A strong hit of good Jewish guilt. I was conscious of the muted noise we made, shuffling across the carpet, the creak of the stairs, but these little sounds—it was becoming clear—weren't going to wake anybody up. It's hard to be at ease in a new place. Home is not the place you own, or even where you go back to. Home is the place whose exigencies you most fully comprehend and can account for. I was sitting on the edge of my bed in the dark. This was Dara's house more than it was mine. She knew it better, and no reason why she shouldn't. After all, she'd spent more time here than I had, or would.

I thought back on our family's old house in Miami, how Dad used to set the burglar alarm before he went to bed. I'd come home late and it would make a long low beep when I opened the door, then I'd have twenty-five seconds to get to the keypad and punch in the code or the siren went off. My brother maybe couldn't admit it yet, but he had to see that some things were better here.

I heard the low flush of a toilet, followed by the still-softer sound of water in the basin of the sink. There was brightness at the end of the hall, then darkness once more. Dara was one moving shadow in a sea of them, barely distinct against the deep blue of my bedroom door, which she had shut softly behind herself. She stood still a moment, in the gloom, then slid into focus as she crossed the room. By the time she reached me she was a girl again.

THE JEALOUSY OF ANGELS

I'd been working at the plant awhile and had hit a kind of
rough patch, but there were also good things, like my girl
June, and I kept telling myself that it would be all worth it.
We were going to make it big, her and me.

Then these angels came, a whole band or regiment or
whatever it is they've got up there. The angels said June's
beauty was unsurpassed by any human ever before or after,
which of course I told them I already knew. They didn't seem
impressed. Thought they were better than me—it was obvious. Then they said she was too beautiful to even live and
that they would take her life. I told them I thought that was
some bullshit.

The Archangel Gabriel related the following:

And God so loved the world, that He gave unto them
His only begotten Son, that whosoever believeth in

Him shall live forever and never die. This made the angels cry in jealousy. And sob, their faces hidden, their angelic voices muffled by the sleeves of their dampening robes. In the absence of their interminable praise-songs it was suddenly clear just how drafty and solemn the high-arched domes of the Heavenly Vault had been built, footsteps and shuffling wings echoed creepily, and the balustrades—gilded and with their Roman columns—suddenly seemed gaudy and more than a little bit lame. This suddenness was contradictory to what Augustine had written about the eternal unchanging nature of God and the old saint, filled with shame, stalked to the far reach of some gray cloudbank where he sulked and remembered how it had been back in the good old days when the Church first aligned with Empire. So a meeting was called, handbills passed out, an ad hoc committee formed to facilitate. Eventually, an agreement with management was reached. The angels would return to their singing and to watching over humans—with a thirteen and a half percent increase in pay and six extra vacation days per annum (the proceedings were conducted partially in Latin, for nostalgic reasons). As well, the angels' union would draft a team of seven (naturally, this being the Number of God) from their membership, and these would go down to earth and take away the most beautiful of all God's beloved humans and that token gesture—it was decided—would reset the balance in the question of who God loved best and then all business as usual could continue for all time, until the inevitable and imminent Apocalypse that is like a slow train coming from a short ways off.

Gabriel made an elaborate, sort of swishy gesture which I took to mean he was finished. Michael was stroking June's hair and sniffing behind her neck. He had big fluffy white wings and tiny little white fangs, which I said I thought was odd but Gabriel said all angels have them. In the far corner of my living room, Satan the One They Call Deceiver had appeared. He had his red arms folded over his red chest, and commented that if the union had been so powerful in his day he might have never left the industry. Then they killed June with their angel powers and her soul poured like holy smoke from out the top of her head and some underling whipped out this contraption like a wet/dry vac and sucked her soul into the holding tank, where it would wait until they got back to Heaven where June would be one with God. The wailing of her spirit grew faint as they passed through the ceiling of the apartment and then the roof of the apartment building. They left her corpse behind and I didn't know what to make of that or what to do with it. I put on the TV.

Satan asked would I mind if he stuck around and watched the news.

A baby had been miraculously saved after falling five stories, when the back doors of a pillow truck burst open at just the right time.

An old Hassidic widow about to lose her home to the bank had discovered, beneath a floorboard, seven hundred thousand dollars in Nazi gold.

The angels, it seemed, were already back on the clock.

The news went to commercial. "Big business, big unions," Satan said, "it doesn't matter. They just want to keep the wheels turning. Screw whoever. What about the guy who invested in all those pillows? Or the descendants of those Nazis? Don't they get theirs?"

"Or me," I said, "and June! Don't we get ours?"

"You can fill out a complaint form," Satan said. "It'll take 'em a while to process it, always does. And it's a pain in the ass. They really put you through . . ." He kind of trailed off.

"Forget it," I said. "I've got enough trouble showing up for work on time."

"That's always how it is," Satan said. "They keep your days filled with the piddling shit so you don't have the time or the heart to go after the big stuff."

"I'm trying to watch TV," I said. "You want a beer?"

And he said okay, and we watched TV, and that was it. God signed a big contract, the angels stole my girlfriend. You cannot petition the Lord with prayer. Me and Satan split a six-pack of Harp. You'd think the whole business at least made me glad to know Heaven was real and that I would see June again there in that city of gold where the roses never fade. But honestly, knowing the truth was no comfort at all. Narrow gate and all that. Like I said, the angels in their fervor had left me to deal with June's body. You think a guy like me knows how to make that sort of problem go away? Who do you think stuck around and offered to help?

GO DOWN SWINGING

David adjusts his stance so that the distance between his feet equals the span of his shoulders. That's the way. He cranes his neck to one side, then the other, really stretching his muscles, loving the tiny pops of the vertebrae. He's imagining: blue helmet, scuffed plastic, padding on the inside worn thin; weird *thereness* of the cup in his underwear; the itchy uniform. He's holding a mop handle. He has the music turned way, way up. He's taking practice swings.

Roger is a good-looking guy, and everyone says that's the worst part. David sort of thinks that's funny, that it says something about how people are, but what he really means is that he thinks he's as good-looking as Roger is, though Roger is a runner, strong, toned, rides his bicycle to work and for pleasure.

Sometimes, when Roger thinks nobody is around, he hobbles out to the porch to smoke a cigarette and have a sob. But David, mop handle on his shoulder while the changer is between discs, can hear him.

A week and a half ago, Roger ate a few doses of acid too many and decided to find out if God existed by climbing onto the roof and asking the moon. After a few hours up there he began to yell. Estrella was pretty sure that some wine would level him out. She stood in the dark yard and cooed. (She was putting herself out, being sweet like this; it was not her nature.) She tried to lure him down with a jug of the bitter merlot they always seem to have on hand. Roger called down that yeah, he probably could use something, but he was scared to try and negotiate the ladder, which kept going staticky like bad TV reception whenever he tried to focus on it. So she brought the bottle up, they sat, and he told her secrets about the moon that were really about a secret love for her, and she touched his hand and turned him down, and they talked about God for a while.

The moon had told him God was real, and that He had selected Roger for a particular mission, but then it had gone silent, and Roger didn't know what he was supposed to be doing. The last thing the moon had told him was that he would need a helpmeet (it had used that particular word, he said) and when he saw her head appear over the edge of the roof he had taken her for a sign, which, he said, he still wasn't convinced that she wasn't. She told him that she thought God was endless, beyond all finite and ultimately illusory constructions such as identity. Estrella is the kind of girl you listen to and want to believe. Roger agreed that God was above all things mortal and physical, but when she told him that this meant that God—who does not play war games—could not have selected him for a mission, he became agitated. She had meant to liberate him from the burden of the impossible, but seemed instead to have driven him into despair.

Had the moon lied? Perhaps the devil was afoot. He eyed her.

She climbed back down the ladder, left him with the wine. Another hour went by. Then the words *I WILL* clarioned in the night, followed by a raucous hosanna that devolved into a scream. David and Estrella pulled out of a kiss, sat up on the couch. David reached over and flipped a light on.

"What the fuck?" Estrella said.

How long has it been since David actually played a game of baseball? The city leagues, the Optimist league. His dad coached teams comprised of his best friends and select hangers-on. He thinks of things his dad would say: *Eye on the ball* or, if he was being too choosy, Dad would say, *Swing! Don't go down looking.* If your swing wasn't even, if it angled down too far, coach would call out, *Hey quit chopping wood out there,* or, if it was angled too far up, it would be *This isn't golf, son!*

He had not loved it, and when he got just old enough for it to become clear who was and wasn't any good, he gave it up, nearly without regret. Had hardly thought about it, in fact, when his father decided to keep on coaching even after he quit. (The old man, in his prime, could have made the minors or maybe gone further, but for whatever reason never tried out.) David realized, looking back, how much it must have meant to his dad to scream at scrawny kids under the bright lights of the city field, his tee shirt ("COACH") tucked into his blue jeans, the brim of his cap crisp; he wasn't a folder. He took all his teams to the playoffs and some to the championship. Well, his dad had never been cruel, at least, as disappointed fathers could be.

Sometimes, David even went and watched the games. He remembers being happy that his father was happy, and thinks, now, with some pride, that this was a pretty grownup feeling for a kid to have.

Roger never did say what he agreed to on the roof, but he'd obviously failed to do it. Now drunk, but still hopelessly high on acid, he crawled across the front yard. He dug his fingers into the ground. He dragged himself forward like a maimed zombie in a horror film.

David and Estrella carried him inside and helped him to the couch, talking—not quite bickering—about who would drive Snapcase's car to the ER. They ignored Roger's protests. Snapcase was asleep. They could wake him up, see if he'd do it, or just give over the keys.

"But isn't he sleeping one off?" David said.

"Yeah, but maybe he's better now," Estrella said.

Estrella told Roger he should ice his foot and he said okay, but then they didn't have any ice. David filled the trays up, came back to the living room. Roger kept insisting he was fine. He hadn't hit his head, right? He'd landed on his feet, mostly the left one, which currently could not bear any weight whatsoever, which was why he'd been crawling. He said that meat was amazing—how weird it was to be *made* of something.

The wine, whatever was left of it, was still on the roof. They sat around and had some beers, smoked a joint—nothing too heavy. Estrella thought Sammy had Percocet but he was out somewhere.

"Think you'll sleep now?" Estrella said.

"Oh yeah, yeah for sure," Roger said. The rush of the jump seemed to have cleared his head. He was no longer talking crazy. Maybe it had neutralized the acid. (Who knew how these things actually worked?) Soon the beer and pot would take care of the adrenaline and he would get some rest.

They helped him into a better position on the couch. He was good and stretched out, his foot elevated on a stack of pillows. (They forgot to check on the ice they were making.) David tossed a blanket his way, and he and Estrella retired to their separate rooms.

Later, Estrella padded past the living room on her way to the bathroom. She wore boy boxer shorts, her black hoodie with the Hüsker Dü backpatch, and a pair of oversize plush

Homer Simpson slippers that someone had scored from the Dumpster at the bottom of frat row. She stopped in the doorway and looked in on Roger. "Y'okay?" she whispered, hoping he'd be asleep.

"Yeah," he said sleepily—then, "love you."

"Night," she said, and shuffled across the linoleum, slippers whispering. She let herself in to David's room.

In the morning, passing through the living room on his way to the kitchen, David saw that Roger was still sleeping. He called Roger's job and said Roger needed the shift covered—family stuff, emergency. A grandma. David still didn't like soy milk in his coffee. It usually separated and got gross. But Estrella was vegan lately, so there was no real milk in the house. He'd have happily stolen some, in order to satisfy his taste without fueling the industrial-agricultural complex, but her reasoning had as much to do with health as economic morality.

He fished around in the cups with his spoon; first his, then the other. No chunks. He'd done okay. He brought the two steaming mugs back to his room.

Roger got a soft cast and crutches. Stay off your feet, they said. He had broken his ankle, the doctors told him, and it had been very stupid of him to wait. If the bone had already begun knitting, he would have to have it professionally re-broken.

They left the ER at sunset, the pink hospital like a part of the sky, a dull spot in the burning pink-orange shot through with blue and some tatters of gathering black. Probably it would storm.

"What am I going to do?" Roger said.

"You'll stay with us," David said. It was the right thing and because it was the right thing he wasn't just saying it, he meant it, too, even though Roger made him feel competitive in a way he could not articulate, for a goal he could never quite specify. It buzzed on his tongue like a sharp mint or a blocked word.

"Of course you'll stay with us," Estrella said. Snapcase was driving, a beer between his legs. There was really no question. They were a family. (Nobody had seen Sammy in days. Maybe he'd hitched upstate, or met someone, or gotten busted, except wouldn't he have called from jail?) Snapcase eased through a red light, then half a block up saw a cop car hiding behind some bushes. It hadn't seen them. He came to a full stop at the next sign, sipped his beer—in his hammy fist it might have been a Mountain Dew.

At Roger's follow-up visit, they scolded him about the antibiotics. They told him that alcohol neutralizes antibiotics, so doubling the dose was never going to do the trick. They told him they'd told him all this the first time he was there. Did he want to lose his foot? Roger cast his eyes down and he was very sorry.

He promised to take the drugs and to not drink, but he

also decided not to pay for the rebreaking of his bone. If it became necessary, he'd have one of the guys do it, *then* go over to the hospital and get it set.

Snapcase wanted no part of Roger's crazy idea. Sammy, who was home again, said he'd do it, but nobody thought he was strong enough. David told Roger he'd think about it. He said it "intrigued" him.

"I mean it's real violence," he said to Estrella. They were in bed. "I guess wife-beaters and psychos do this kind of stuff all the time."

"And cops."

"Right. But those people are so fucked up they don't even get it. That it's like this totally *there* thing. This leg. A person. Totally nontheoretical. The Real."

"David, those people *live* in the Real. And so, in fact, do we." She drew him into the aura of her warmth. "You poor theorist," she said.

David tells Roger to put up the cash for the bottle. That's only fair. The whiskey is for courage, partly, but not really. David is looking forward to this. He wants there to be a bottle because to swig whiskey before swinging straight and true seems proper in a grand sense, like knowing just how to act at a funeral or during a riot.

When the new disc settles into the tray and starts to spin, Roger's snuffling and hitched breath disappear. Social Distortion fills the world. A guy they know plays in a weekend league and he's bringing a real bat over when he gets off work, but for now David's still swinging the mop handle.

After his friend drops off the bat, David sits and holds it, gingerly, as if it were volatile or imbued with magics. He's imagining Roger's bone shattering and how it will feel to do a righteous violence. Estrella says Roger seems depressed, and she's going to bunk out in the living room with him tonight. Okay, David says. Probably it's nothing. Even if it's not nothing, still okay. Stretched out diagonally on his bed, luxuriating like a king (when she's there they sleep in a sweaty tangle), in his mind he deals blows that have Roger screaming through his bite-rag. Like an expectant father with a wife's overnight bag packed and ready, David has carefully washed a single tube sock. He keeps coming back to what Roger said on the night he hurt himself. That word. *Meat.* If all goes well he won't actually see the meat. Still. It is so red and shiny in his mind.

The swelling is going down. Roger says maybe they should wait another day. David says he thinks they've waited too long already, but Roger says he feels different, somehow. He's always known his body's rhythms. He feels a rally.

Estrella tells David it's obvious something is wrong. Can he just fucking spit it out already?

"Perhaps," he says, "it might be I'm jealous of the attentions lavished by women on the nobly enfeebled."

"Oh Christ." Estrella rolls over and away from him. "Who's that? Barthelme?"

"No, but isn't it pretty to think so."

"Fucker," she says.

He grabs her shoulder, pulls her toward him.

"Oh," she says, still annoyed, but intrigued. "So that's how you want to play tonight?"

When they take the cast off, the leg is shriveled and the muscle sags. The black hairs press into the skin. He looks like the recipient of a graft. The doctor uses the word *miracle*. David finds such word choice unprofessional, as well as, frankly, a bit excessive.

Roger becomes reinvested in the devout Catholicism of his youth. He moves back into his own place, starts going to Pax Christi meetings, works himself back into shape. They seldom see him anymore.

But sometimes, when David wakes up early enough, he'll spot Roger out on his morning run: sweaty, renewed. Probably Roger is oblivious to the figure in the window. Does he ever give a thought to what he stole from David when he was healed? David tries to make himself forgive Roger, but he just can't. After a while he doesn't even want to.

"I mean you *know* I would never—"

"David."

"I—"

"Just *stop*. Just shut up and let me look at this."

Estrella is at the bathroom sink, her right arm over her head, her left hand touching her right breast, prodding it to test its sensitivity, studying in the mirror the crimson bite mark on its underside. It really didn't bleed that much; a bruise is all it should have been. The skin breaking was a total accident. It's the middle of the night, another night. David, silenced, finds himself reflecting on how rarely they do anything during the day.

"Baby," he says.

"Don't," she says. "I mean it's okay, it'll *be* okay, you know whatever, but right now just don't."

FINDING MYSELF

I keep finding myself in places I don't expect me, such as outside churches, lurking, peering in their dooryards, or inside my own hollow skull, living a life to which the term *hardscrabble* might be astutely or ironically applied. Luckily, there are no ironists or astuticians around to subject me to application. It's just me in here—I'm not even wearing socks. A warm footness buoys faceward. Sometimes, I positively swim with aromas. When charming certain women this everyday household constraint can be recast in the light of advantage. Conscript your drawbacks into tempting signposts of your touchable personhood: it's the only way, and in this way do I obtain access to *their* definitive admixtures. I'm concerned though that the footness has been preserved—uncharmingly—in the fabric catalog of this secondhand armchair, already overstuffed with records of what it's been to whom. A casual observer couldn't separate the come stains from those of the breast milk. No matter; we're talking about poles of the same basic problem: the punitive fact that I am not a casual observer. Of the few things I do well, casualty is not one of them. I'm the guy who clenched his teeth. Do you remember him and me being him, how you wished we would have moaned instead or called your name out like a concise indictment? But that's not us. We're intense and idio-syncratic, just like everyone. We love out of fashion. We call exes in other states just to chat. We're comfortable with your new man, really, we just don't want to hear about him. We want instead to tell you about the weird time I found myself headed in opposite directions on the east side of Sixth Avenue between West Eleventh and West Twelfth, on our way to and from the red express train, wearing the same shirt. I didn't recognize me right away. It took us some time. We knew I knew me but we wasn't sure, and so stood there trading platitude futures while we plumbed every inner depth, searching for what had to be there. Each of us trying to remember our name, force it first onto the other one.

SOMEWHERE I HAVE HEARD
THIS BEFORE

Stan was eleven years old and things had gotten so bad between his parents the only thing they could agree on was that he should spend some time out of the house. Since it was coming on summer anyhow, they packed him up just like they'd done in years previous for camp, though this year there was no money for that, no way. They sent him instead to his aunt, his mother's sister, a distracted woman, twice divorced, who lived in a decent house on Long Island in a neighborhood the long-time residents felt was in decline. *Changing* was the word they used. They were mostly Jews and what they meant was blacks were moving in.

Aunt Lisa had long blond hair, split at the ends and graying at the roots. She lit purifying candles, was a sort of New Ager, and had a boyfriend who owned a landscaping business. They smoked pot up in her bedroom, where she thought her daughter and nephew wouldn't smell it, though both of them did, though only the daughter knew it for what it was. Mandy was fifteen and totally grunge. She hated her mother for a hippie and she hated summer because it was too hot to wear the clothes she liked to wear (she wore them anyway) and because she was in summer school because she'd spent the school year stoned, which is why she had her mother's number, all right.

Aunt Lisa's boyfriend's fortunes were declining with the neighborhood's. It was because the new neighbors did their own yard work. Nothing too fancy, just a simple clean yard was what they liked: grass mowed, hedges clipped, done. And for the most part they did it themselves. He talked about his troubles over dinner. "Niggers," he said—he wasn't even Jewish—and Aunt Lisa said "Charles," and that was that.

Stan was in love, obviously. Mandy had an angular face, boy hips, missile tits, and natural red hair streaked fuck-you blue. She wore torn black jeans and thrift-store tees that advertised defunct products or commemorated the company picnics of yesteryear. Sometimes she would pick out a plain white shirt and scribble some band's lyrics on it with a laundry marker. And always the red-and-black flannel, worn unbuttoned all the way (cuffs too) so the outsize shirt hung on her like a drape. She kept her wallet clipped to her pants with a long shiny chain that she was hopeful would scuff with time.

Stan sat in the living room in the big chair by the picture window, sometimes holding a comic book, sometimes nothing at all, staring out at the street waiting for that first righteous glimpse of her on her walk home from summer school.

Naturally, she had him totally figured out and some days called him a baby and sent him off and so the days when she felt like putting up with him were extra special for them both. On those days she treated him like an equal, sort of, and took him down to the basement, which had been converted into a den by the first husband and decently appointed by the second.

Aunt Lisa had inherited the home from her mother. Aunt Lisa's sister—Stan's mother—had gotten the cash and Aunt Lisa had gotten the home. Aunt Lisa had never had doubts about who got the better deal, especially seeing as how Stan's parents had pissed theirs away. The house still stood and still was hers. Men came and went, leaving their improvements behind as testament to the degree and duration of their best intentions.

There was a TV in the basement den and a nice comfy couch and a pool table even. Mandy would put on MTV just to have it on but she didn't like to watch with Stan, who asked too many questions and didn't *get it*. Having to explain why things were cool made the fact of their coolness less certain, and certainty was the rock on which she built. He was a summer baby, would turn twelve there, but in the meantime she didn't need the grief. What he needed to do was learn.

They would stand behind the pool table, in the farthest corner of the basement, where there was no view from the stairs, where Lisa or Charles would come from if they ever came down to check on them, which neither ever had nor ever would. Mandy put her cool hands inside Stan's clothing and touched him all over. "Let's see what's going on here," she'd say. Or she'd put his sweaty hands inside her clothes and when she did that she said, "I'm going to teach you something today. When you're older your girlfriends will thank me." This was a variation on something a boy at her school—a senior—had said to her the previous winter, before teaching her something she hadn't exactly wanted or not wanted to learn.

Stan didn't understand how Mandy would know his girlfriends for them to thank her, since he didn't actually live on Long Island. Wasn't he going to get to go home—back to his familiar school and shouting parents? Maybe if he got married one day there would be a wedding and everyone would come. Mandy might go up to his bride on his wedding day and say, "You better thank me for what I taught your husband, Stan, back before you even knew him, that summer he stayed at my house." Anything was possible with Mandy, who smelled sour in a sort of good way and that was only the tip of the iceberg of how she was strange. He tried to imagine what the thing he touched looked like based on what it felt like but everything he thought of seemed insane. It made no sense for anything like what he was thinking to be a thing that was a part of a person.

So he asked if he could see it. She said she'd show him, but that if she did he had to kiss it. He didn't want to do that so he never saw. She got angry and called him some things that he didn't know what they all were—but he got the gist anyway, and some of them he did know—and she stomped up the stairs. He stayed behind the pool table and cried and felt bad about everything, like what had just happened and Mandy being angry with him but also how he missed the predictable madness of his fucked-up parents and also news headlines that scared him and other stuff, too, vague huge stuff, because it had gotten to the point where it really was everything at once.

As he calmed down he began to hear the TV again. It had been on the whole time but he'd tuned it out for a while. It was reentering his life like a shuttle back from space. They were doing a special on a rock star who had killed himself in the spring. There was some footage of a crowd gathered in what looked like a park, and then they played a song by the rock star's group. The dead person was the singer, and he dressed, Stan saw, sort of like Mandy. Distortion churned from the amplifiers. It was aggressive, messy music, but weirdly catchy—like someone had taken a Beatles tune and transcribed it for chainsaw orchestra. Stan thought that the rock star screaming was the most pure sound he had ever heard.

When Stan was seventeen he dressed like Mandy had when she was fifteen. Now Mandy had short spiky shock-white hair and raver pants. She was in college and had a gruff doughy girlfriend. Charles and Aunt Lisa had gotten serious, but never married, and in August Charles had died of a brain aneurysm. Now it was the High Holidays. Stan was staying in the basement. Same old couch, but a new TV. His parents were upstairs, in his mom's old bedroom. Aunt Lisa wasn't much on synagogue. "I'm spiritual, but not religious," she'd always say, with cautious certainty, as if coming to the realization for the first time. But this year she fasted and even stayed at services through Yizkor.

They all broke the fast together at sunset and then the older folks went to bed, so Stan, Mandy, the bullish girl-friend, and Jeff—Charles's son from a previous marriage, who Aunt Lisa had *insisted* join them for dinner—decided to go down the road and have a drink at the Hi-Tone, where nobody ever got carded. "I think I started coming here, like, the school year right after that summer you stayed with us, Stan," Mandy said to her cousin. "If anyone else says they're sorry," Jeff said. They were a few rounds in. "I mean, it's not like I don't believe them, I mean of course they are, but how much can you take, you know?" He seemed to be waiting for one of them to answer him. When they didn't, he said he was going out front for a smoke and the girlfriend asked if she could bum one and went with him. Mandy and Stan sipped their beers.

"I *am* sorry, you know," Mandy said to Stan after a while, "about." Then she didn't say anything. She looked up at the front door. But then she looked back at Stan. She said, "I mean it was kid stuff. Stupid."

Stan didn't know what he wanted to say, or what he was going to say, though he knew he was about to say something.

The truth was he hardly ever thought about the summer he had spent playing touch with his punky cousin. He was older now than she'd been then. He'd slept with a few of the girls and one of the boys at his high school and was mostly happy. His grades were nothing special, but then neither was he.

"Is Darcey a heavy sleeper?" he asked her. Darcey was the girlfriend. He thought about the words he'd just said. He thought to himself: *that's what I just said.*

She said nothing, only stared ahead. Was she mad? Had she even been listening? He didn't like her staring like this. He touched her leg under the table: the knee and then the fullness of the thigh, then his hand was floating in space and that meant she had either jerked away or opened for him, he didn't know. He finished his beer in one long pull, then stood up. He had gotten tall. He fished a couple quarters from his pocket, went over to the jukebox and punched in the number for his favorite song of all time, which he supposed she'd recognize. He couldn't decide if he was changing the subject, making some grand statement about it, or just doing whatever he wanted. He went up to the bar and ordered fresh drinks for everyone. The other two would be back any minute. It was a cheap place but that hardly mattered. His parents had gotten their shit together and he could have sprung for that round of drinks if it'd cost twice, three times what it did.

It wasn't his play on the jukebox yet, but all he had to do was wait. All he could do was wait. When he heard the opening chords—certainly, at the latest, by the bridge—knowledge would rise up inside like water seeping into a basement or an unfurling rose—or better yet, it would arrive in his mind fully formed, ex nihilo, like how when somebody calls you with the bad news your first thought is always "I already knew that, I have always known." The words a lie at the moment you first think them, they immediately become true and stay true forever, just like the lyrics to any song.

WHAT WAS ONCE ALL YOURS

I was a few months shy of eighteen when Ma got religion. Hard to say what changed for her, exactly. I used to blame her father's death for it, on account of how devout he was his whole life, and raised her himself. She took his passing about as hard as a person can. But I don't know that I ever totally believed that explanation, even though I was the one who made it up. Maybe what makes more sense to say is I never believed it was the full reason, and that what I really think is this: sometimes deep down in a person is a switch waiting to be flipped, and nobody knows it's there, not even the person, until one day—flip. And whatever light that switch controls pops on, starts to shine.

It was church every Sunday, all of a sudden, and some weeknights. Socials. Bible study. Whatever there was to do down at the church Ma meant to do it and have us all alongside her. The God stick whacked her so hard it seemed to have shook her brains loose, and I took to thinking of this as her "condition."

First it was the Baptists, which was bad enough, but that romance proved short-lived. Ma joined the Assembly, and not one of us—Dad, Kyra, nor myself—was prepared to follow her there. So she let it be known that anyone who failed to join her in prayer would like as not fail to join her up in Heaven, and could hardly step out to the Walgreens, much less the church itself, without shouting up from the bottom of the staircase about how it might be the last time we ever beheld the countenance of one another forever.

Dad left a note that said we could reach him down at his brother's in Corpus Christi if we needed to, and that he'd send some money when he could, but the gist was good-bye and good luck. "You're old enough to understand this," said a part of the note that was addressed to me. I still don't know whether I think that's so.

With him gone, it was as if her last anchor to earthly things had been cut, and her condition quickened. She was crazed, fervent, and implacable—a real banshee for Christ.

It's scary when a person you have always known becomes a raving stranger before your disbelieving eyes. But there was nothing I could do. Time passed—crawled along, it seemed like—and I had my birthday. Legal finally to vote, smoke, and buy porno—not that I had a lot of interest in the first or much keeping me from the other two. I had my job at the grocery store and there were girls, Cass mostly, and drinking at the lake with my best friend, Joe Brown. Between all that and school I was hardly home, and Ma tended to go after whatever was right in front of her, so I was spared a lot, though on occasion she'd dial me up on my cell just to say that maybe I thought I could fool an old woman but there was One whom I sure could never fool.

All I ever said back to her was "Ma, you ain't so old."

My sister had a harder road. Ma used to just about torture Kyra, who was extra pigheaded on top of what comes naturally with being fifteen—that age when your situation seems like a life sentence, so you always act like you've got nothing to lose, but also no hope of ever winning.

Kyra took to rebelling, and snuck out and got caught sneaking in and shoplifted and got herself kicked out of the high school and generally drove Ma to distraction any way she could, which for a time seemed to about make them even, until the night Kyra nearly died. Fistful of downers some boy told her were a real good time. Probably he'd hoped to feed her a couple, maybe diddle her with his fingers after she passed out, but she swiped the whole bottle from his backpack and brought 'em home. Joke on him, right? Me and Joe Brown found out who it was from her friends, went by his place and had a *long* talk with him, you can bet you. But that's not this story.

Like I was starting to say before, I was spending a good bit of my time with Cass. She was junior to my senior at the high school, a chicken-legged brunette with acne scars on her cheeks, hairy forearms, a perfect behind. She was a known slut, and the most serious student in our whole school, for she understood that grades could be a ticket out, and was only ever stumped by one question, which was why nobody else seemed to understand the same. She had a decent singing voice but didn't use it. When we did it drunk she liked to be called things.

Cass encouraged me to keep up with my schoolwork, but if I didn't—I didn't—that was my own lookout. She let me hang around while she was working, so long as I didn't put the TV up too loud. I liked this arrangement. I liked to be right there when she finished with her studies. "Okay," she'd say, closing the day's last book, and I'd look over her way, grinning, knowing it was finally time.

Which brings me back around to Joe Brown, one of maybe three guys in our school who Cass hadn't ever fucked, or at least rubbed off in the lunch room through his jeans just for something to do. Joe Brown was breathless around Cass. It was stammering, moon-faced love. He didn't have to hide it from me and made no effort to, even though she was my girl. That's the kind of brothers me and Joe Brown were.

"She don't even know I exist" was the type of thing he'd say about her, which was obvious garbage since everyone knows everyone in a high school, besides which shit towns like ours don't have strangers. In fact she knew him plenty well, and couldn't stand him. She was disgusted by his love, the sight of how she made him weak. She figured he'd eventually harden himself up or die a victim of his own witless yearning, and she expressed only the mildest curiosity—certainly no preference—about which one it might be.

Knowing all this about him, and about her, there was truly only one thing I *could* do, which was to describe in perfect excruciating detail every moment of every instance of my penetrating Cass to Joe Brown while we drove around the lake road, drinking our beers. It broke his heart to hear these things, and made him nauseous with longing, but if I'd stop he would beg and beg for more. He didn't know it, and it didn't seem to be exactly working, but I was giving him tough, fierce love, which is the best kind. I wanted to see him beat this thing. I did not want for him to spend the rest of his life a sweaty mouth-breather who made girls laugh uneasily, shake their heads, and walk away.

We didn't have money to buy more beers, so we went to Joe Brown's uncle's place, where there was always a selection. His uncle's name was Connie, but everyone called him Judge, since the night several years back when he got in a bar brawl that ended with him head-stomping an out-of-towner who'd been accused—by Connie, mind you—of looking down his nose. "Who's judgin' *now?*" he screamed over and over at the man who was bleeding and curled up fetal on the floor. Cost Judge his badge, but earned him his nickname, and probably we were all better off with him having the one and not the other. Judge loved his name. He loved his nephew, and let Joe Brown come over and do as he pleased. This was very lucky for Joe Brown, and therefore for me, too, because Judge was a bad man. He even kept two women, who wore stretch pants and had lousy blond dye jobs. He was quick to beat either. One had a pair of identical boys, nine or so years old, and they were considered fair game, too. He listened to the kind of talk radio that makes your brain shrivel up like a salted slug. He hated Jews something awful, but respected Israel for its military balls. To sustain decency for five consecutive minutes would have been beyond his capacity, besides which he didn't have two friends in ten who'd have known it for what it was. He ran a sideline business selling illegal fireworks, was the kind of man who'd swerve *toward* an animal in the road, and generally speaking he needed nothing so badly in this world as to be run through with a great hot knife.

Judge has nothing to do with this story. He wasn't even at home. We let ourselves in, swiped a six-pack from his fridge, and went back to Joe Brown's. Judge is simply a character on whom I can't help but dwell some. Something pulls my thoughts back his way. He inspires a loathing so pure, to be silent about it seems no less a crime than denying love.

So we were at Joe Brown's, down in the basement, which was his room, drinking Judge's beer. My phone buzzed. I almost didn't look, since I wasn't going to answer anyhow. It was bound to be Ma on another psycho Jesus tear or else my damn sister wanting a ride home from some party out in the sticks. But then I realized it had been just one buzz, two pulses, like, *he-ey,* and so I looked. It was a text from Cass: COME OVER RITE NOW.

I showed the phone to Joe Brown. "Now what do you suppose this could be?" I said.

"Shit," he said. "How am I supposed to know what that girl's thinking? I'd give anything to get inside her head." This was just a little yearn, a passing thing, like a stringy cloud. And yet I could not let it pass me by.

"Well," I said to him, "maybe you need some inside perspective. Like do something she does so you can think the way she thinks."

"Yeah? Like what?"

"That's easy," I said. "I can't even believe I never thought of this before."

"What, Troy? What is it?"

"Well Cass's just about favorite thing in the whole wide world—"

"Yeah?"

"—is sucking me off. So you better get to it."

"Aw, you motherfuck," said Joe Brown. He looked punched, then gathered himself and lunged forward to punch me. I hopped up from my seat and out of his range. We were both laughing. I hated and loved myself. I got us a couple of fresh beers. They hissed our truce. I flipped the phone open and dialed.

"Are you on your way over?" Cass said. I'd been planning to kid her for a bit, since I was already on a roll. I figured she was just looking to hook up, and there was no reason that couldn't wait—let her get even more worked up, right?—but I knew as soon as I heard her voice that kidding was the last thing on her mind, and that sucked the kidding right on out of me. "I'm a little drunk," I said, "over here at Joe Brown's place. What's up?"

"Then buy a coffee," she said, "on your way over. And do not under any circumstances bring your girlfriend along with you." She was gone.

"All right, honey," I said into the dead phone. "That sounds real nice. I'll be there just as soon as I can."

Well, I had knocked Cass up.

"Well," I said. We were sitting in her driveway in the front seat of my car, cold half-drained cup of coffee on my dash, so she could see I listened. Her house was dark, folks inside asleep, and I was thinking of a way to say that wasn't it possible it hadn't been me who'd done it—who'd been the one—and it seemed to me that such a thing *was* possible, only I couldn't think of a way to say that, but she figured out what was on my mind and gave me a look I could not help but read correctly. "I mean," I said. I said, "Shit, Cass, forget it. Forget it. I'm sorry."

"If you don't want to help me don't help me," she said. "I'm smarter than you anyway, and I've got more money. So make up your mind real quick and if you're gonna be in then be in."

"Cass," I said, and took her hand, which was closer to me in both of mine.

She said, "Well, okay then." And we sat like that a while, her crying some.

When it seemed right to, or at least okay, I asked what was it she thought she'd like to do. I was trying to speak carefully, because I'd fucked up and hurt her feelings once already, but also, I was feeling oddly mixed about the thing. Terrified, yes, but also something else—excited, I guess, even somewhat thrilled. Like being on the edge of a cliff and thinking, *Maybe if I jump I'll fly.* If we did it, it would be something we could never take back. I looked with a mingling of fear and true desire upon the idea that I might be forced to become some kind of man. What if I worked hard, raised myself— us—up? A small family out on the lake on a fine day in high summer. A boat of our very own.

"Do?" Cass said. Her tears were dry. "You know the answer to that, if you think you know me at all. Shit. I got a *life* ahead of me, not this."

I was swept through with a blessed relief so sweet I'd have lost my feet if I hadn't already been sitting. My fantasy crumbled like the pages of an old brittle book. *Oh Dear Christ Jesus Rock Savior Master King,* I thought. *Oh Merciful God of Heaven, I am no more fit to play daddy than jazz trumpet, and I thank you for leading this girl into wanting to kill our baby. Amen.*

I promised Cass she was not alone in this thing—promised up and down till she believed me. So the next day I set out to prove it, and went down to the library so I could get online. I never visited the library much, but I liked it. It was small and not pretty, but had a sort of built to last quality. Its architecture did not bespeak a shame about its own existence, which seems to be the traditional style for community buildings.

I learned there were only two places in the whole state we could go. It seemed to me that this miserable figure held a glimpse of some deep truth, like the world loves nothing so much as to make a hard thing harder, but of course I knew it was no natural order but fence-swinging Christers with their big ideas who had made it this way. They were people, I thought, who treasured denying mercy and bestowing pain. Self-appointed fixers. My own mother in their swollen ranks, drinking their decaf coffee and trifolding their newsletters. Belting their tuneless hymns.

I went outside the library and called the number, talked to some woman who was formal with me, but kind. She wouldn't let me make the appointment for Cass, but gave me information I could tell her, the most important piece of which was that even though the Lifers had about run abortion out of the state altogether, they had somehow not managed to get passed any of that parental consent and notification stuff, which meant that whatever else happened, they couldn't force Cass to ask permission.

Because of where we had to go, the only way it made sense was for us to take a weekend and make the trip. I told Cass about having to make her own appointment, and other stuff I'd learned, then I booked us a room at a place the woman on the phone had recommended. Cass wanted to pay half but I said no. She told her folks she was going to visit some friends who were freshmen at State. I got my shifts covered at work, and told my mother that me and Joe Brown were going down to the Gulf to fish on the boat of a guy Joe knew. I told Joe

Brown he was my cover for a hot weekend me and Cass had been planning that also included a second girl, some friend of hers from Jackson who looked mighty special judging from her MySpace picture, and so whatever else he did to make sure and not let my mother see him hanging around town while I was gone.

Hurting him with the truth was one thing. This was a different case. Extreme and necessary, yes, but Jesus. I could hardly lift my head for the weight of my guilt.

We lit out early, and it was a good drive. We talked, but not too much; she studied. I never did understand how some people can read in a moving car. There were protesters outside the clinic. This had not been unexpected, but was still a fairly great shock to see. These people in their mad devotion. Old men with liver spots held up posters depicting things no less horrible for being mostly obvious fakes. Young people in their church bests. Enormous middle-aged women with short haircuts and fanny packs, heavy necklaces of colorful unprecious stone. The day was genius with sun, the kind of day that makes you want to say, God bless the sunny South forever, and not even be kidding at all. A man in a cheap suit stepped into our path and I let go of Cass's hand and stepped out in front of her.

"Where are these children's parents?" he shouted. Not to us, but past, addressing his own cohort, re-proving whatever it was they were all so sure they already knew. Cass, behind me, closed a hand over my fist and squeezed. I knew she would never forgive my fulfilling what was right then my life's one dream of seeing this weasel's blood run down my knuckles. He looked about my father's age. I let my hand slacken, and walked forward, leading her on. For a second I thought he was going to force me to walk into him, and if that happened it would be all bets off, for my patience was expired and Cass did not have the power to stop me twice. But the weasel was only playing chicken. He dodged.

She was woozy after, like the doctor had warned. He'd said that would last the day, and that there'd be some bleeding. All normal. I picked us up cold sandwiches and juice, so we'd have them if we wanted, then took us back to the room and made sure she was comfortable and asked if she felt like talking. I told her I had been scared for her, even though there'd been nothing to be scared of, really, because I'd read all about it beforehand and the folks there had told me, too. I told her she'd done the right thing, that *we* had—I wasn't sure which was the correct one to say, or which way she preferred to hear it, if at all.

I told her she was the smartest girl I knew, maybe the all around best one.

"Those people are just sick," I said, thinking again of the weasel, his pinched face with its lightless eyes. Cass said something, but it was muddled, and may have also trailed off. I thought I heard my name, but didn't ask her to repeat herself. She slept, and didn't wake up until the next day, during which same time I spent eternity wide awake and all alone.

• • •

I wanted to show her how nothing was changed between us—I hoped and was determined that it wouldn't be—so late in the morning I woke her with a delicate stroking of her breasts, and then, as it was made clear that what I was doing was acceptable, I kissed a straight line from the top of her forehead and between the eyes clear on down to her thicket and buried my face there gently. Her fingers in my bed-frizzed hair. Neither of us finished. Finishing wasn't the point, not this time, and knowing that made me feel like we were both of us older than we had ever been before. But then, in the bathroom, in the horrible motel light, I stared at the reflection in the mirror and felt like a stupid kid. A not unwelcome sensation. I had blood smeared on my lips and chin like some gnarly animal. I was wild-eyed, pasty-pale, with dime-size nipples and a shitty sprig of hair that didn't nearly cover the space between them. I looked at this bedraggled figure and knew it as myself and saw myself seeing myself and knowing myself in this way, and I got started laughing so hard my whole body shook, and Cass came in to see what the matter was. I couldn't tell her, didn't know how, but it was enough, I think, for her to know that there was cause for laughter. She joined in, then grabbed me by my unabated hard-on, aimed it at the bathtub and set me free.

This is not to say everything was okay, painless and sweet every moment thereafter, only that it was those things right then. And that we deserved them. We showered together, stood beneath the hot stream, took turns washing each other's backs. We checked out of that awful, rundown place and started back a day early toward our shit town, which, it turned out, had let our absence pass largely unmarked.

The world is not brimming over with grace, but it does have some.

There's no great conclusion to me and Cass. We were bound by something that could neither break us nor lift us up. It did not make us other or better than we were. Why should it have? I took her to senior prom, which was real nice, and we sometimes talked about loving each other or being in love, but we were using the words just to use them, like practicing for when we'd really need them sometime in the future. I knew she'd gone back to messing around on me and I never gave her grief about that. After I finished school I had less patience for her studying, and we sort of both started to move on, though I always said hello when I saw her now and again, at parties, usually, except for the quarter she spent in perfect seclusion, studying to retake the SATs and boost her score into the very top percentile, which she damn well did, not that I was surprised to learn it. Soon enough after that she was gone. We became ourselves, is what happened, and whenever I miss her I remind myself of that. But don't think this is a story about true love gained and then lost forever, because it's not like I think about Cass often, and many times even when I do I don't miss her at all. I'm happy for wherever she's got to, if it's anyplace good.

Joe Brown at first didn't understand. He knew it was different between me and her, somehow, but his main concern was the fact that I would no longer tell him dirty stories about Cass McElroy's sweet, sweet pussy that never got sore, or even say anything about my hot threeway.

He kept on pestering me.

I finally called him a fucking deviant to his face about it, one night in the sick grip of summer, when it's so hot people are only living to find new ways to bring hate into the world. I thought of the weasel who had stood in our path, and put everything I'd had for that man onto Joe Brown, which wasn't right, but it's what happened. We had a fist fight, real serious too. Came out bruised, bloodied, and sore—more brothers than ever. Joe Brown might not have had a way with girls, but he lifted and he ran. He was strong. Whipped me, if the truth is to be told about it. A year later he said he had decided to enlist, and three months after they sent him over he was gone. He was in an unarmed Humvee, driving it, in fact, down a desert road and rolled right over an IED. We buried what they sent home.

And Judge should have died the night his trailer's electric hookup faltered and sparked a whole box of M-80s, which set off a thundering like a movie drive-by and sent the whole place up. He was spared on account of not being home, though the mother of the twin boys and one of the twins were there, both asleep, which further suggested that Judge had been playing at his version of family man before slipping out to get away with one more damn thing. The other boy, who had gone to have a sleepover at a friend's house, now lives with his aunt's family in Baltimore, and Judge lives to rave and spit for another season. He may outlast the rest of us yet.

But I don't want to finish on a down note, so since I didn't tell the rest about how it turned out with Ma and my sister and the drugs, let me get back to that now.

Ma found Kyra puking up all over herself, her bed, her room—and then Ma. There was an ambulance. Stomach pump plus IV drip. A three-day stay at the hospital and then six months of mandatory counseling sessions to see if she was lying about the accident and had maybe done the thing on purpose.

They say He works in mysterious ways. I used to not know what that meant but now I do. Not to say whether I believe it is the true case, but I understand what it means and why people say it. The aftermath of this ugly episode was a cleansing effect upon our household. Holding her own daughter's head up by the hair, wearing the vomit, slapping the girl to keep her conscious until the ambulance men came—all these things got Ma a little bit more invested in the soul's particular vessel here on earth and in earthly things in general. Not to say she didn't take Kyra's surviving for an obvious miracle, but still. Caring for her recovering daughter woke up her natural instinct to be kind. It shook her condition loose.

Kyra, meanwhile, in the midst of her close call, in her near-death state, saw the Lord, and He told her some things that set her to rights. Belief-wise, each got knocked a few pegs in the other's direction. If my old man ever came back this is what I would show him: his daughter and the mother of his daughter, how they are like sisters now. I would say, Forget everything else, this here is what you lost out on. This is what was once all yours.

Ma and Kyra, thick as thieves, go together to First Presbyterian, and if you do not engage them on the topic of queers or of Democrats you will see that they are good Southern women, full with love. I swear they mean the world no harm.

TETRIS

Jennie is sleeping when it comes but I'm awake, in my underwear, face slick with sweat. Our air conditioner has stopped working. The brownouts had been ongoing for about a month when one day—*zap*. Too much starting and stopping, I guess. At least the power's flowing right now. The TV and the Nintendo, I am thankful, still work. The Nintendo especially is a miracle on account of that it's so old anyway.

The sunlight is indirect—our house has good tree cover—but the temperature is high. Jennie's naked. She is tall, solid, pretty, and currently not speaking to me—I mean she wouldn't be if she were awake. We've been arguing lately because she says I don't do anything but play Tetris anymore and I always ask what the fuck else would she like me to do. Sometimes she picks up the Bible and thumbs through it. She doesn't know this, but I stole that Bible from a motel, one night way back before all the trouble started. Weird lights in the sky and nobody sure what was happening, if it was God or the government responsible, i.e., who to blame or praise. The book is inscrutable to her, though she's become steadily more convinced it is trying to tell her something. She's mad at me because I took a few religion courses in college but I won't help. I won't even look at the damned thing. Earlier today I told her (again) that I studied Islam and modernity, not Christian anything, and that if she wanted to go loot a Koran from the already ransacked Books-A-Million down the street, then I would gladly give her my class notes and term papers when she got back.

It was a cruel comment, I knew even as I said it, but it did what I needed it to do—truncated the discussion so I could play this game, which has muted colors and I can mute the music, thus exercising forms, degrees, of control. I lose at the game when I get caught up staring into the background— that radiating black that can be generated only by a back-lit screen. Or when it gets just too fast. When I lose the game the screen fills with candy-colored snow.

Jennie said that between the two of us I have more experience with religion, even if what I know is basically about something else. *At least,* she said, *it's something.* And when I still wouldn't take the soft-sided white book from her trembling hands she called me a whole string of bad names and curled up on the floor with it, beside the couch. She cried into the ball she'd made of herself and once I tried to stroke her hair but she wouldn't be touched so I just sat down close to her and fired up the game. Eventually she fell asleep and her breathing is the only sound in this room, along with the tiny sexual slaps of my thumbs on the plastic buttons.

Snow again. I lose. This game is designed to end, not to be beaten; I doubt they even programmed a graphic for the YOU WIN screen. Once you hit level eighteen the pieces are falling almost quicker than hand-eye coordination can trace, and it can go faster and faster. It outlasts you.

I play again and at level eighteen reach a sort of ecstasy of self-and-game where we are as close to becoming one being as we ever will and this lasts some amount of time and then ends. Snow again. I enter my initials on the high-score screen, ranked number one. The list erases every time you shut the Nintendo off.

Outside the window there is a fiery brightness that fills the world, a limitless wave, jellying up the street towards us.

When people think about the Apocalypse they imagine knowing what it is that will bring them down. Ask the shades of Hiroshima about that one. The assumption of knowledge is one part of the fantasy of mastery, by which I mean the hope against all damned hope of survival. I never thought about what time of year the End might come, but looking back, I guess I always figured it would be in the crush of summer. And I was right.

I watch Jennie, whom sleep has loosened from her furious ball. She is stretched out across the floor, and how beautiful she is. I wish the world wouldn't end before we could make up and die holding each other.

I glance out the window at the bright wall. It seems closer, but slower. I notice the watch on my wrist and the clock on the TV have both gone to 88:88. I wonder what that means, if it tips the scales in my mind concerning who/Who is responsible. When it occurs to me that Jennie will most likely die in her sleep I almost wake her but then I don't. I am calmed by watching her steady breathing and there isn't time to reconcile anyway, what with the way she gets when she's sulking. I'm going to let her sleep through it, through whatever exactly is out the front window, reclaiming the driveway, the sidewalk not dissolved but disappeared. For all its luminosity, the wall is not painful to look upon—it is oddly soothing. It leaves no trace or shadow of what is behind or within. It is perfectly opaque. I see it the same way that Jennie sees the Scriptures, and also like Jennie, I get madder and sadder and madder again, but I won't look away.

A HOUSE IN OUR ARMS

We made it to New York.

That's how we put it when we talk about it with each other, even though it means something different to each of us, and even though we're both pretty used to it by now. I came straight from school, worked some crap jobs, then landed a decent one. It's at a hedge fund and I hate it, at least theoretically. In practice I find the more time I spend doing it the less I feel one way or the other. It's just what I'm doing, what I do. I work with nice enough people. They started me out as an assistant but I'm already almost a junior manager. Who knows where I might wind up if I stick around?

Leah stayed on in our college town, waitressing and getting fired from waitressing. When she got tired of that she moved home for a while, then traveled. Europe of course, and the Far East. Now she's studying sculpture. She talks about getting "my MFA," as if dropping by the school to pick up something she left there, maybe a coat.

We never dated, of course, but what we had—there's no exact name for it—was well understood and envied within our circle. I mean the other guys sometimes would ask me what it was like to go to bed with her. She was the recently turned lesbian they all wanted to be the one to turn back. And how smug was I? How quick—but also truly pleased— to explain that I was the exception that proved her rule. Ah, college.

I suppose we are still enviable, since what we have is the same as it ever was, though probably most of the people I know now wouldn't envy us.

Leah is in a new version of our old world, but I don't worry too much about losing her. We have the fullness of our history to draw on. We see each other as often as our schedules allow.

I'm supposed to be going with her to an opening tonight, and I've been looking forward to it, but I get held up at the office and have to send an apologetic text message canceling on cocktails but promising to meet her at the gallery.

Because of this, Leah greets me curtly and then rejoins the little semicircle she was in when I tapped her shoulder. A group of people all about our age are standing around a rotund, gray-haired man who I believe has an essay in the current *New Yorker,* which I subscribe to, though if he is who I think he is then I fell asleep while reading his article. To show her that

I am other than a perfect philistine, I spend several minutes studying what is clearly the star piece in the show. It has this monumental physical presence and a sort of explosive personality, like Rauschenberg covering Nevelson, or vice versa. *See?* I say to the Leah in my head. *I know a thing or two about this stuff.* The Leah in my head is very impressed.

I glance across the room. She's still doing her thing over there. I go for the refreshments: a long metal table with jugs of wine and lightly sweating pyramids of cubed cheese. I am pouring myself a burgundy when an older man holds out his clear plastic cup.

"Fill me up?" He smiles suggestively, but with more than a touch of self-awareness, maybe even self-parody. I laugh and accidentally shake the jug a little as I pour, spilling a few drops onto the man's hand, but thankfully I don't stain his cuff. "Oh," the man says. "Now you'll have to lick it off."

Am I going to laugh at this? He's laughing.

Okay I'm laughing.

We laugh.

Richard has a full head of salt-and-pepper hair, and is thickset in a way that suggests how he'll go to seed, but also that he hasn't yet. He prides himself on the fact that he can be *scandalous,* "but hardly after two cups of bottom-shelf merlot," he says, and I remind him it's burgundy we're drinking and Richard laughs in a way that is almost shrieking.

After a quick turn up and down the gallery, chatting, we come back to the table for refills. The burgundy is gone. Now we really *are* drinking merlot.

Leah comes up to us, rosy, buzzed, ready for my attention. Richard drifts off. Leah wants to point out Alison, the conceptual portraitist she's been seeing but is currently on the outs with. I can't remember what happened this time. There's always some particular incident—the ostensible reason—but at bottom the fact seems to be that there is a natural ebb and flow in the women's ability to tolerate each other. But there is real love there, Leah is certain.

Alison is heavier than I expected, with curly dark hair and sad eyes. She looks Jewish, and is deep in conversation with a much older woman who I think is the reason we're all here.

You know what I mean when I say that.

Leah is saying good-bye to the famous critic and I am throwing out our cups, thinking about how long it will take to get home and what time I have to be up for work tomorrow. Is it early enough for a nightcap somewhere? If we hurry. I run into Richard at the garbage can.

He insists I take his number, which he's already written down on a napkin. "Just think about it," he says, placing one hand firmly on my shoulder. "You look like you could use someone to make you a real dinner. A growing boy like you. Really, anytime."

So sometimes I have dinner over at Richard's.

It's a different night. We're leaving a bar, up by Leah's place again. It rained while we were drinking and the city looks delicate, refreshed. All the streetlamps have birthday-candle haloes.

Leah is hanging on my arm. It's no big thing. She's not stumbling, just making sure I feel her presence, her *there-ness*. We reach her building.

"Gentleman you are," she says. "Walking me home."

I smile.

"So you want to come upstairs?"

She slips a hand into my pocket, squeezes.

"Well," she says, "what's it gonna be?"

"If you really need me to say it," I say. "I mean of course."

"Awesome," she says, and pecks me on the cheek. Hand still in my pocket. "But you're not staying over."

But then she lets me.

I live in Murray Hill. Leah lives up by her school. This means that in order to see her I need to take the 6 to Grand Central, ride the shuttle to Times Square, then finish my trip on the 1. Or spring for a cab. Not that I'm so broke, but still.

Richard has a rent-controlled place in Alphabet City. The neighborhood, seedy when he moved in, has gentrified smartly over the decades. Richard has stories about the prostitutes who used the corner Laundromat (which has since become a coffee shop) as their home base, about the bums who would sleep in his building's stairwell, ready to fight you if you roused them, about how all the real *character* has been driven from the city, though it *is* nice to be able to walk around at night.

A cab home from Richard's is eight bucks, tops, and often Richard *insists* that I take some money to pay for it. "Refuse me twice and you'll make me cry," he'll say, half-serious. (It's sometimes hard to tell with Richard what is genuine and what is theater.) I act exasperated—you're making me feel like a kid, I say—but accept the cash, grinning, and only then can we complete our good-night ritual: a hearty, pro-tracted embrace during which he pecks me on the cheek, or maybe tries to plant one right on the mouth.

I've begun to crave the undivided affection Richard gives me on our nights together. Sometimes when I'm at work I find myself drifting off, thinking of the low light by which we dine, how he's taken to keeping a bottle of my preferred bourbon in the house. "I don't know about another round *before* dinner, Richard," I might say, and Richard might say "Oh come *on*— you young people are supposed to be able to take it."

It's hard to say who's more surprised the night I respond to Richard's latest hysterical come-on by stretching myself out on the couch and then laconically unzipping my fly.

I no longer think of Leah as the love of my life, but I do still sometimes think we might make each other the happiest. It would be more like teaming up than being married. We could do all kinds of things together: whatever she wanted to. I could work, she could sculpt; she could have girls too if she wanted. She could bring them home to us sometimes.

I know it's silly, but I think about it.

Also I think maybe it isn't so silly.

I'm imagining the two of us at a party together, her wearing a black dress with a plunging V neck, me not in anything particular, and she's talking to some old friend of ours. She's telling a funny story about something I said on account of having misunderstood something she said, and how we argued until we realized what the original miscommunication had been, and how afterward everything was okay.

Richard fucks with a ruthlessness utterly disconnected from his demeanor, that carefully crafted mélange of snark and fey. He tops, for one thing, and sometimes when he gets frisky he gets rough. The situation ought to allow for nothing in either partner but animal instinct. Instead, I'm feeling oddly trapped inside what is shaping up to be a muddled, but essentially analytical, drunk.

How have I wound up in this apartment, on my belly, on this bed, greased?

Obviously I don't mean this literally, but in the grander sense.

Richard's trying to get me into position for a reach around, but I'm not helping because at this particular moment my being fucked feels like it is happening in an adjoining room. In that room, I think, Richard has given up on parity and is now calling me filthy things.

The smoke alarm goes off. The salmon. Richard pulls

out. It is a rushed, painful exit that makes me gasp. Richard runs to the beige disk and snatches it off the wall, disabling it. He opens the oven and surveys the ruined food. The salmon is blackened and hard; it looks like scorched warped bricks.

"Goddamn, goddamn," Richard says. I hear the quaver in his voice.

We stand at opposite ends of the kitchen, two naked men, first not looking at each other, then looking.

I am eating fried pork dumplings out of a white box balanced on my lap, a lot less drunk than I was before, which I think is good. Richard has spareribs and makes a show of sucking the meat off each bone. I start to tell him all about Leah, figuring there is an obvious segue from that into breaking up with him, but I can't find it, so I just keep telling old sex stories.

"Ugh," Richard says finally. "I ate a pussy once in college. That was *plenty*."

"I think we should be just friends," I say. Richard stares at me, gnawing on his last rib. "Okay, I know it sounds stupid," I say, "I mean we're sitting here and—" I make a sort of encompassing gesture with my chopsticks.

Still, Richard says nothing.

"I don't want to hurt you. Really. But this is a mistake for me. I thought maybe it wasn't, but it is. I hope you can understand. We can still see each other. I love it when you cook dinner."

Richard clears his throat, starts to talk, stops, then says: "You know, I try and remind myself that you're all the same, but apparently there are some things in life a person never gets used to."

"I don't understand."

"Of course you don't. You're trying so hard to be understanding but the fact is you couldn't possibly understand. You apparently think that you're my boyfriend. You think *this*"—he mimics my gesture—"is my whole life."

I let Jason from the office talk me into letting his fiancée, Danielle, who works in legal, set me up with her good friend Candace. In an e-mail CC'd to Jason, Danielle sends me Candace's e-mail address, along with a short note explaining that Candace is recently out of a long relationship and probably won't be looking for anything too serious right off. I write to Candace, who I've been told is expecting to hear from me, and reintroduce myself. (We met a couple months ago at somebody's birthday party, but that was before she was single.) She writes me back a few minutes later, saying she remembers me, and in my next reply I ask if she'd like to get together some evening after work for a drink. She doesn't write back for a few hours; in fact, I'm getting ready to leave the office when she does, though since she wrote to my work e-mail—the only contact info of mine that she has—it would have forwarded to my BlackBerry if I hadn't still been at my desk. She says she's looking at her schedule and next Wednesday works for her if it does for me.

We have a good time.

• • •

I'm in Leah's kitchen, which is also her living room. We're sitting in high-back wooden chairs, getting drunk on Maker's Mark. I guess we're about halfway there. Her apartment is an almost uncramped studio near the park. At least the tub is in the bathroom. Recipes are stuck to the fridge with fruit magnets, though Leah only ever eats out or orders in.

She's been telling me about this studio class she's taking called Across Mediums: Conversations Within and Between the Arts. It sounds interesting, or at any rate she seems to be enjoying it, and like evidence supporting an alibi, here's a copy of *The Collected Poems of Frank O'Hara* on the table. It's thick, paperback, black; the cover dominated by a yellowed headshot of the poet. He has close-cropped dark hair, a high forehead, full lips. He's looking over his right shoulder, gaze brimming with a melancholy not entirely unsweet.

I open the book, flip to a random page, and read what I find out loud:

"the unrecapturable nostalgia for nostalgia
for a life I might have hated, thus mourned

but do we really need anything more to be sorry about
wouldn't it be extra, as all pain is extra"

"Don't be afraid to jump around," she cuts in. "That's the way to read him, my teacher says."

So, on another page:

"if Kenneth were writing this he would point out how
    art has changed women and women have changed
    art and men, but men haven't changed women much
but ideas are obscure and nothing should be obscure
    tonight
you will live half the year in a house by the sea and half
    the year in a house in our arms"

This time I interrupt myself. "Who's Kenneth?" I ask.

"I'm not sure," she says. "He's always mentioning people. You get the feeling they're all somebody. There might be notes in the back." There aren't. She gets up from the table. I put the book down and finish what's in my glass.

Leah's got her head in the freezer, checking to see if the new ice is ready. I get up from my chair and go to her. I grip her hips, momentarily, then slip my hands around her front, get underneath the fabric of her tee shirt, and clasp them over her belly. Holding her close against me as chilly air washes over us.

"Hey there, you," she says, and presses back.

I circle her nipples with my index fingers, feeling myself tense as they tighten.

She turns her neck to the side, as if yielding to a vampire.

I kiss her on the neck, then pull her closer still—I want her to tip her head back so we can kiss.

"Couldn't this be it?" I say, speaking the words into her hair. "Isn't this good enough?"

She reaches behind herself, thrusts one arm between us and pushes. Her other arm drawn across her beautiful breasts like a shield.

Leah doesn't throw me out, but she also doesn't try to hide that I've upset her and how badly. We can't talk about it, or I know she won't so I don't even try, but it's what goes unsaid between people that builds up like masonry. You have to either knock the bricks out with other things, or let them keep stacking until eventually you are alone in a room. So the important thing is that we are sitting here, together, sharing a silence that is both charged and cozy, working on a fresh round of drinks.

When they're finished, Leah doesn't offer to refresh them again. She says she thinks she'll get ready for bed. I wobble a bit when I stand. We say good night and I see myself out. We have always forgiven each other everything. It is easy to believe that we will survive love.

Leah's building is on Amsterdam and 108th. There are subway stops on Broadway at 103rd and 110th. Does it make more sense to walk north to the closer stop or walk the extra five blocks south and have one less stop to ride?

I'm walking down 108th, toward Broadway, not knowing which direction I'll turn when I get there. Then, instead of turning one way or the other, I decide where I really want to be is inside this bar on the corner. I've never been in here before. I take a stool at the far end, order a Maker's, shoot it, then order a beer to sit and sip on, though before I know it half of that's gone, too. It's pretty busy in here—a student hangout, apparently, though of course that can mean a lot of things. The Pixies are on the too-loud stereo. Straining to listen to the conversation nearest me, I am able to discern the word *epistemology*. English majors.

"Do you know what *time* it is?" Richard says. "Of course you don't or you wouldn't be calling." I'm on the sidewalk in front of the bar. "So. How drunk are you, exactly?"

I say, "Nobody knows me like you do. I don't understand it." I'm not even slurring too badly, all things considered. "What did you mean when you said we were all the same? Who?"

"Christ," Richard says.

"I'm not a fucking TYPE Richard I'm a fucking PERSON."

"It's not one or the other, Todd. You're a type *of* person, and I'm sorry if that hurts to hear, but it's true. Also, I'm not that sorry. You typed me right off as a needy used-up old fag, and now that you know I'm not you're trying to recast me as magic negro to your plighted hero."

"Fine, okay, you're right. Everything, you're right. So okay, fine, hit me with it—what am I? Type me."

"You," Richard says—dramatic pause—"are the type who hears the deadbolt turning but can't tell whether the door is about to be opened or has just been locked shut."

A taxi is sailing up the street. I stick my arm out. It sees me, pulls an outrageous U-turn in the empty intersection, sidles up to the curb. "I'm coming over," I say to Richard. "I'm going to make it right between us."

"No you're not," he says.

"I am," I say. "I already gave your address to the driver." I put my hand over the mouthpiece and give his address to the driver.

"It's already right between us," Richard says, "in the sense that it's never going to be anything other than this. You try to make things better, and that's sweet, sort of, but the fact is they aren't yours to change. I'm sure it's the same with your other—situation, though *please* don't take that as an invitation to start talking about what'shername."

Richard hangs up, but only because he's a showoff, and needs to always have the final word. He's in love with the sound of his own voice cutting out, and imagining what that absence sounds like in my ear, but by the time I get to his place he'll be out of his snit, and ready to be good to me. He may even offer to pay for my cab.

WEEKEND AWAY

Steven's calling. He does this once or twice a month, depending how things are going for him. Three times means *pretty bad*. We haven't had one of those in a while. If he ever called four times I might be worried or curious enough to pick up.

My phone buzzes in my pocket, rings if it's on the charger, and I'll look at it and see it's him and not answer. I haven't spoken to him in ten and a half months, which I prefer to think of as a year, since we are coming up on our one-year "anniversary" anyway. What he does is leave a voice mail and then not two minutes later call again and leave another, so each "call" is actually a pair of them: binary stars.

You can imagine what a hurry I'm in to go retrieve these messages. Sentimental reminiscences, mostly, slurred by drink and tending toward the graphically sexual. The rare wild plea for another chance.

I do love knowing how deep in him I run, still. My lasting power in and over his duplicitous heart. That in the depths of his misery this is what he comes back around to: some vision of me that makes him throb.

He stirs things up in me, too, that's true, but I can endure what I feel when I hear his recorded voice in my ear. At this point, the urge only serves to further chasten.

I am something of a stoic, these days, and Steven lives down in Sacramento with the woman he left me for.

Sometimes I wake up in the morning and my first thought is how funny—and *funny* is the right word—it is that I probably will never see him again.

We will speak, sooner or later. Even though I know I shouldn't pick up the phone—and to my credit, so far I haven't, not even once—the fact is that one of these days I will. I'll pick up the phone and say hello to him and then—what?

But probably we will never again meet face-to-face, in real life.

I mean, if I knew he was going to be somewhere, I wouldn't go.

Real life. What a funny concept. When I think about it—This is *it*! Happening! Now! Andnowandnowandnow!—there's nothing that can keep me from bursting out laughing, sometimes until my sides ache. If he could somehow see me in that state he'd get a sort of nostalgic look on his face and take this tone he has, the one that on the surface says, "I'm feeling wistful" but really means, "Pity me and submit." In that tone he'd say, "*I* used to be able to make you laugh that way," and then I'd say "Oh, but Steven, don't you see that you still do?"

"They call it Rose City," he said. "This place was made for us."

I was in Florida, where we're both from. I was living with my mother for a while and starting to not believe myself when I would repeat my mantra: *You are* not *moving across the country for this man.*

"I mean, it's your goddamn *name*," he said. "How can this not be just perfect?"

I forget whether that was the conversation when I said all right, here I come, or if I didn't fully cave for a while longer.

Enough. It is a new day, bright and crisp, and I will not waste it dwelling on old bad memories. I drive a car with a top that goes down and I'm getting in it and I'm going. I'm gone.

But I do want to say one more thing about it. Steven is the one who left me. That's true. But it doesn't mean I didn't sometimes think about leaving him, because I did. I had even started to look, in a hypothetical sort of way, at the different neighborhoods in the city and try to figure out which were the ones where I could afford something decent on my own and also not have to cross paths with him much. (This, obviously, was before I knew what his plans were.)

I didn't once think about going back to my mother's, or to Florida at all.

It's March. The sky is clear and the air is still cold. Too cold to keep the top down for long, but I will for awhile. I don't care. I always hated the hot sticky Floridian wind. Keep your swamps and outlet malls. If Steven did one good thing for me—and there *was* plenty of good between us, even if I don't think about it much—what he did was get me out of Florida.

Thanks, Steven.

Right when I wish for a hitchhiker I get one. Maybe it's my lucky day. I should buy lottery tickets. I see him from a distance and slow down so I don't overshoot him. I sidle right up, a pro at this.

"Hey there," I say. "Been doin' some hard travelin'?"

"I thought you knowed," he says. I love him already. His black, messy hair mostly covers his ears. He's wearing dark skinny-fit jeans and a brown tee shirt with a stencil of a broken machine gun on it and the all-caps directive to MAKE LEVEES NOT WAR. There's a hole in one of the armpits of the shirt. He's five-seven in his boots.

"Come on, get in," I say. "There's a whole mess of discs without cases in the glove box. Woody's in there if you can find him."

"Or we could plug in my iPod," the hitchhiker says. "I've got a car adaptor cord in my bag."

•   •   •

Bruce is nineteen, a student at the visual arts school in Portland, and trying to get to Tolovana Park. All I know about that place is that it's the next town south of Cannon Beach, which is where I'm headed.

I ask him if Tolovana Park is where he's from. No, but his mom lives there now. She runs an antiques shop in Cannon Beach that does most of its business during tourist season, which officially kicks off Memorial Day weekend. She sent him money for a bus ticket, but he spent it all on art supplies. Later, after we've spent some time riding and sung a few songs together with Woody, he reveals that the school provides him with most any art supply he could ever want and what he really spent the money on was pot.

We're on the Sunset Highway, US 26 West, half an hour past Staley's Junction, where I picked him up, so about halfway to where we're going. Out here, the highway is a two-lane road, cut into the earth in such a way that on some stretches the bases of the huge trees are at eye level on both sides.

Bruce digs around in his pack and produces a little wooden pipe and a film canister. As soon as the canister is open a marshy green sex smell fills my car.

I steer with one hand and hold the pipe to my lips with the other. I let Bruce work the lighter for me. I draw in deep, then break out in a coughing fit that pops the cherry from the bowl and shoots it into Bruce's lap. He lets out a surprisingly girlish noise and starts swatting at himself. My eyes are squeezed shut tight with coughing and I accidentally swerve the car hard left, wait for the sensation of the crash, remember there is nobody else on the road anywhere near us, then feel a different sensation, from underneath the car, realize that while I am still going more or less in the direction of the road I have now gotten off it entirely and am driving in the grass, which, thankfully, is flat here and not some runoff ditch or something.

I force my eyes open, pull back onto the shoulder, bring the car to a stop.

"Holy shit," I say. "I am so sorry."

There's a small scorch on Bruce's jeans about mid-thigh.

"Where's your mom's shop?" I say. "Is it open? I'll drop you."

"You want to have burgers or something?" Bruce says.

We go to the lobby restaurant of the first beachfront hotel we come to and I decide this will be my hotel for the weekend. There are a row of them up and down the beach, most still closed for the season. We are the only people in the place, but I think it would feel vast even if it were full. The ceilings are too high. The windows that look out on the beach must be ten feet tall and half again as wide. I wonder if I'm the only guest. I mean, if I will be after I check in.

We are ravenous and make short work of our burgers. We pour so much ketchup on our fries they get soggy and cold. That's okay. They're good that way, maybe better. Two refills apiece of our Cokes.

When the bill comes Bruce goes for his wallet.

"Are you kidding?" I say, and pluck the check up off the table.

"Listen," Bruce says. "Let me come up to your room with you."

"Bruce, I think it's time we get you home."

"But I'm all gross," he says. "From the road. Let me take a shower and change my clothes."

I don't know what time it is. "Your mom," I say. Bruce bursts out laughing and can't stop. I don't know how long the laughing lasts, only that I'm laughing too. The light in the room is thick like soup. It looks the way pot smells. Pot smells the way it feels inside you. The way it feels inside you is the way you feel in the ocean. The way the ocean feels, all around you. It is still too cold to swim in this ocean. I came all the way out here just to stare. "No," I say. In my head: *Jesus, complete the thought.* "I mean, won't she be worried. I mean, I'm sure she is worried."

"I don't think it honestly matters," Bruce says.

You can pretty much always swim in the ocean in Florida. Even when it's as cold as it gets it's still not nearly as cold as it is here.

"Why are you doing this?" I ask Bruce. "You've got this place to go be and you want to be there, I mean you put all this effort into getting there, but now you want to be here."

"Why shouldn't I want to be here?" Bruce says. "You're pretty and we're having fun. You know, you haven't even asked why I'm going home."

"Why are you going home?"

"I'm not telling you," he says. "It's nothing good, that's

for sure, but it's also nothing that can't wait a day. Does that make sense?" He's packing another bowl as he says this.

Does that make sense? Does it *not* make sense?

Doesn't it have to be one way or the other one?

Well—does it?

I'm a late sleeper. I always have been. I heard Bruce stirring and though he was quiet I heard the door open and click shut behind him. I did not rouse myself. I drifted back down.

As a parting gift, I see now, he left me a single expertly rolled joint on top of the pad of hotel stationery on the nightstand. Sweet, sweet boy. I get dressed and go to the sea.

I'm wearing two sweaters. It's about noon and icy and gray.

I have the joint with me but no lighter or match, not that either would stand much of a chance against this wind coming off the water. I sit down in the sand. When my rear gets too cold to sit anymore I stand up, brush the damp sand off myself, then wander down by the edge of the water and look at the anemones clinging to the sides of rocks, the little fishes trapped in tide pools and the crabs. They scuttle up out of the sand, then over it, down in again somewhere else.

I turn away from the sea, cross the dunes, go around the side of the hotel, and come to the Cannon Beach main drag, such as it is. I walk. Most everything is closed, except convenience stores attached to gas stations. Oh here and there a shop is open, but there's nothing I need or that so much as interests me, at least until I come to a little place I am sure is the right one.

It's warm inside and musty, packed to the gills with—stuff.

I had pictured the sort of establishment that deals in well-kept relics, things people knowingly overpay for because they're just *perfect* for that empty space on the wall opposite the guest bed, or the mantel over the fake fireplace. This isn't that at all. What this is brings the word *rummage* to mind. There are weird recovered castoffs in various states of completeness. There are wooden baskets full of paperback bodice rippers, covers stripped. Unmatched dishes and glasses, beat-up pots. Bolts of fabric that look at least a decade old, priced not by the foot but by the bolt. On a low shelf, about waist high, a wooden stereoscope rests atop a pile of cards for it. I don't lift the thing up to try it out for fear of breaking it, but the top picture—two pictures, really, but identical—is of Portland around the turn of the last century. Beside it stands a ceramic figurine, maybe a foot tall: a crow with a jaunty smile and a black top hat that matches his feathers. A bow tie below his chin turns his folded wings into the suggestion of a tuxedo jacket. I think I will buy this for a present for Jack.

This is the first I'm mentioning Jack. I know that. He's the guy I've been seeing since a few months after Steven left. He's a strong, tender lover and a good man. I have this problem where whenever he's not around I forget he exists, until some random moment when I remember that I'm not just a wronged lonely woman and in fact am loved by somebody, somebody in every way better—anyway, better *to* me—than the person I lost. The heart can be funny but the mind can be even funnier.

Funny is almost certainly not the right word.

I put the crow down on the counter next to the register. I ding the little silver service bell. "One second," calls a voice from the back room, and then a tallish woman emerges from behind the curtain. She has long graying red hair, masculine shoulders, and wears a pair of horn-rimmed glasses she might well have found among her own stacks, unless she bought them new, say thirty years ago.

She keeps one hand on the figurine as she rings me up, and strokes it gently, the way you would a small tired dog. I put my hand on top of her hand and give it a squeeze.

"You're Bruce's mother," I say. Her eyes go to slits even as they zero in on me.

"Who are you?" she says.

"Oh, I'm sorry, I didn't mean to surprise you. I'm a psychic, actually. When our hands touched I knew you had a son named Bruce."

"You expect me to stand here and take this?" she says. "Who the hell *are* you?"

"I'm sorry," I say. "I shouldn't have said anything. But it's hard being psychic. You get these bursts of true insight and then nobody believes anything you say. I know I'm right. If I wasn't right you wouldn't be looking at me like that."

"Well, if you're so psychic what else can you tell me?"

"It doesn't work that way. I can't just—well, there's something bad that's happened in your family recently and Bruce has been deeply affected. He's trying to be strong for you but he isn't sure if he's strong enough. You should be patient with him, and kind. Does any of that make sense?"

"None," the woman says. "I don't have a son named Bruce."

Back at the hotel, I smoke the joint like you would a cigarette: just keep taking drags until the whole thing is gone.

I get myself into a lot of trouble, going overboard like this.

Sometime after the last glints of sunlight slip below the horizon I realize I'm bored staring out at dark water, and then I realize that this is actually a normal, coherent thought, and this makes me think maybe the worst has passed. I think I'll go down to the restaurant, order something not too greasy and a coffee, then check out and start back home. A nice night drive. Become nothing but a pair of headlights cutting swiftly through the silken dark. Mmm.

What can I eat that won't be too greasy?

Some kind of sandwich, which would also go well with the coffee. I want lots of mustard, so much spicy brown mustard that everybody in the place can smell it and they all gawk, and if there are no other customers to gawk then only the waiter will, and I am more ready for this coffee and sandwich and drive than for anything I have ever been ready for, even as I feel myself slipping off to sleep, curled up in the chair there with the bed so close but also far away and the last thing I realize is having not decided between smoked turkey and roast beef.

Bruce is in the room with me. He's over by the bed, pack slung over one shoulder and his whole form—body, clothes, everything—is incandescent, flickering like old film. "Hey," I say. "I thought I saw your mother today."

"I don't have a mother. I'm not even a college student, just a traveling kid. Here's what happened: I woke up early this morning, took forty dollars out of your wallet—you can check if you want—then walked back to the highway and started hitching again. A man in a light blue '89 Dodge van with no windows picked me up, took me to some lonely place he knows about, messed me up pretty bad, and then left me there. I died. Also, my name isn't Bruce it's Malachi."

The ghost gives me this look of ultimate affection and some pity, like he's sorry how fucked up this is but it's all in perspective, or would be if you could see it from where he's standing.

"Of all the people to visit," I say, "why me? Or is it more like you've got some list and I'm pit stop number whatever."

"You're the one who wanted to be psychic," Bruce says. Now he's laughing at me. "Look Rose, I'm sorry I made up that story. I'm not really dead."

"You promise?"

"Oh yeah, for sure, though the thing about my name *is* true. What actually happened was after I left your place I tried to shoplift some breakfast from a gas station candy rack but the cashier saw me and there happened to be a cop nearby and when they searched me they found some other stuff I didn't tell you about, and now I'm in county lockup, two towns over, and even though you're not a psychic, it turns out that I am. I'm visiting you via astral projection, which sort of makes my body look like it's having a low-grade seizure on my cot, not that anyone's checking. Anyway, I've come to tell you I accidentally left my iPod in your car and I'd really like to get it back, though I guess they won't let me have it while I'm in here so I don't really know what to say."

I give the ghost my phone number. If he ever calls I'll know this wasn't a dream.

"Thanks, Rose," he says. "You were really good to me."

"And yet you left without so much as good-bye."

"Rose, don't make this about Steven."

"I didn't tell you about Steven."

"Yeah but ghosts know everything."

"But you're not really a ghost, right?"

"Well, I've got the psychic thing going for me too, now. It's complicated. Look, I didn't ask for any of this."

I remember now how young Bruce is, ghost or no, psychic or no. And I'm not calling him goddamn Malachi. "Nobody asks for anything," I tell him. "Every day of your life is getting something you never asked for."

I wake up and my mouth feels like it's stuffed with old wool. It's dark, but I don't know what time it is.

Late or early.

The phone's ringing. That's what woke me.

Bruce? . . . Steven? . . . Jack, actually. Worried, I'm sure, or maybe just a bit put out, since we haven't touched base in a few days.

I wait until the ringing stops. When it does, I shut down the phone. It chirps out its little good-bye song.

The problem is now I'm awake.

I put the TV on and some all-movies all-the-time channel is showing *Touch of Evil*. Commercial-free, no less. (Lottery tickets.) It's at one of the parts where Janet Leigh is alone in the room at the motel in the middle of nowhere.

Instead of drawing obvious parallels, I take the longest shower you can imagine. Hottest, too. I leave the bathroom light off but the door open and the TV on. Marlene Dietrich tells Orson Welles his future is all used up.

I turn my face into the stream and feel the drops beating against my eyelids like rain on windows. I open my mouth and let it fill with water and swallow and then do it again. I shut the water off, wrap myself in a towel, sit down on the edge of the still-made bed, and watch the rest of the movie. It's the last scene, where Charlton Heston is walking through the river, holding the tape recorder up to keep it dry and then Orson Welles hears his own recorded voice echoing off the stone arches of the bridge, then the big shootout.

Dietrich again: "What does it matter what you say about people?"

She has all the best lines in this movie.

·   ·   ·

"But I didn't tell you the last part yet," I say to Jack.

"Okay," he says, "hang on real quick while I load the drier." It's Tuesday night. We're back at his place after a nice dinner, and it's looking like I'll stay over. There are some things I left here on another occasion that I can wear to work tomorrow. Jack tossed my items in with some laundry of his own, so they'll be fresh and clean.

I'm telling him all about my weekend away, except for a few things about Bruce that I don't tell.

"Okay," he says when he returns from the other room.

"Okay," I say, and give him back his spot on the couch so I can snuggle up to him once he's settled. "So I'm on the way back home.

"I don't really need to stop but I guess I just want to. It feels more like a trip when you do, and otherwise the drive isn't that long. I'm sipping on a strawberry soda I bought from the machine at the rest pavilion, sitting on a picnic table—not on the bench at the table, but actually on the tabletop itself, with my feet on the bench.

"Maybe ten feet away there's another picnic table. They're both poured concrete, gray, with dried bird shit and old graffiti and everything on them. Anyway I'm alone at my table but this other one's full. A whole family. Mom, dad, three kids, plus another adult. An aunt I guess, mom's sister or else dad's. That's what I decide while I'm watching them. Oh, and also that one of the kids is hers, though I can't tell which. They're all six of them eating sandwiches and spooning out chicken salad and potato salad from these plastic containers, passing things around, eating cubes of watermelon from a big Tupperware. It's warmer off the coast, but still pretty chilly. They're all in jackets and sweaters, having this kind of summer picnic while dressed for fall in the middle of this cold spring, and I think that's part of why I like watching them. They're apple-cheeked but getting through it. Nobody is even complaining that I can see.

"Now the one woman is wiping the kids off and loading them back into the family minivan, which looks like a rental. The man is helping, so I decide he must be that one's husband. The other woman is cleaning up the lunch things all alone. She stacks up the dirty paper plates, gathers up the plastic utensils and puts them on top of that stack, then pops the lids back on the containers of food.

"The garbage cans are up at the pavilion, so she has to walk past my table. I'm finishing my strawberry soda, holding it straight up to get the last of it. She pauses before me. I put the can down on the table.

"'You want some chicken salad, ma'am?' she asks me. 'There's quite a bit left over.'

"I'm looking at her, silent, like I'm thinking, and I am, but what I'm thinking isn't about her at all. I'm thinking to myself that when I get back on the road I can either go back to my life or I can turn out of the rest stop into the north-bound lane of traffic and just go. I know you don't like hearing it but it's true, that's what I was thinking. There are so many places I've never even seen.

" 'It won't keep,' she says. 'We're not taking it with us. It will go to waste.'

"It actually looks like good chicken salad, and I *am* hungry, having left the beach late that morning without eating first. All I have in me is strawberry soda.

" 'I saw you watching us,' she says. 'We're good, clean people and I know this is what you want.'

"And she's right, but I still don't move to take the food. I don't know what it is, and I guess I'll wonder about it for a long time. I mean, I'm not scared of germs, strangers, or anything. So why can't I let myself say yes?"

JEWELS FLASHING IN THE NIGHT OF TIME

+

Summer, 2004

+

I loosen my grip on Andrea's neck and tell her, If you were with me I'd only hurt you when you wanted me to and she says, Then what would be the point? Her voice is a shred. She clenches around me like a raised fist when I cut her air supply again.

A different day:

I'm thinking about that song "Debaser" by the Pixies and repeating the chorus under my breath while I work— "debaser, debaser, DEBASER, debaser"—which I guess doesn't sound like much, but you've got to imagine it the way I do, which is with a melody.

•　　•　　•

Or that's what I hear whenever Brendan walks into the store. Chords fill the air, ooze like oil from a slab of deli meat. It isn't like angels singing and little pink hearts floating around my head or whatever. It's more like I'm imagining his theme music. We both hate the classic rock that 101.9 plays, but it's the only station our crappy radio gets. And that's a lame thing to hate, probably, but it's what we have in common, and it is good, finally, just to pass minutes with music—any kind—because in silence you fall out of time. No. It's the other way. You don't fall out, you fall in. You get stuck, like running through a field and you twist your ankle on a rock. And you just lay there.

So he walks in at the start of his shift while I'm pumping the meat slicer and sort of thinking about him. He's in the mix, let's say. The slicer is converting a length of capicola—long as my arm and nearly thick as both of his—into sandwich-ready slices of the same.

I'm pumping the meat slicer with my right arm, catching the paper-thin rounds of capicola in my left hand—both hands gloved—and tossing the slices with measured gestures. Flicks of the wrist. Each little disc into one of three piles. The boss calls them stacks, but that's because when he does this it all stacks neatly. When I do it there is a mess and when I'm finished the slices of meat make tall zigzagging decks that sway like skyscrapers and need to be straightened before they can be wrapped in clear plastic and put away in the cooler. The decks get shuffled smooth and perfect, like the space of skin between Brendan's navel and the waist of his skater pants. He's maddening, constantly adjusting himself or stretching his arms all the way up so the bottom of his shirt pulls up, his pants slung so low, the better part of his boxers is exposed, but even the underwear doesn't go any higher than his pale bony hips. How old is he? It almost doesn't matter. He'll look fifteen until he's thirty.

Leaving work:

Maybe I'm whistling that song again. Down the street a little ways a man standing at a collapsible table is signing people up for credit cards, offering tee shirts and cheap Walkmans as a signing bonus, wincing in the relentless sun, mopping his forehead with a hairy forearm. I scribble gibberish on the form and take my little radio. He calls out to me that I didn't show him a driver's license, or something else he needs to verify something else. And also that I took his good blue pen. I ignore him and cross the street.

My thing:

I like to read out loud. I know *Story of the Eye* practically by heart but fuck that because holding the book is what's so good. It starts to get heavier in your hands as you work up to the moment when it is time to put it down. This isn't a fetish like I can't live without it. I just mean that it's so good. The words fill you like water and they reach deep into you like a surgeon would. And nobody loves it like Andrea does. With nothing but Bataille between us I picture our minds over-bleeding like the heart of a Venn diagram. I could pin Andrea with a phrase if I chose carefully enough, but that would compromise my favorite conception of her—as a shifting mystery that dances and rings like a wealth of glass, shattering. She's my Simone. That is, when she's not off somewhere with goddamn motherfucking Will.

At the library:

I stake out a back corner with *Heart of Darkness* and my new Walkman. It has those little buds that go right in your ear. I thumb through the wavelengths, past the classic rock, over now to AM, searching for Rumsfeld. *And this also, said Marlow suddenly, has been one of the dark places of the earth.* I guess the juxtaposition is heavy-handed, but whatever.

I can't find Rumsfeld, but some radio personality is reading a list of the atrocities depicted in the photos that have surfaced, in the videos and other photos that are as yet only rumored. Images of horror, and their clinically disinterested annotations, fly across wires and airwaves; the electronic pulses and micropulses like the steady beat of flapping wings, and I imagine storks bearing the names of unnamed methods, dropping each into the fore of the mind where it lingers for just a moment *like jewels flashing in the night of time* (thus Conrad) or *a world where gestures have no carrying power, like voices in a space that is absolutely soundless* (thus Bataille).

I flip to the end pages of the book, the blank part, fish the credit man's pen from my jeans pocket, and start to copy down the list as I hear it: these are the activities with which the poor or underachieving tiers of my graduating class have lately been, in the name of God and country, filling their days:

> Punching, slapping, and kicking detainees; jumping on their naked feet; Videotaping and photographing naked male and female detainees; Forcibly arranging detainees in various sexually explicit positions for photographing; Forcing detainees to remove their clothing and keeping them naked for several days at a time; Forcing naked male detainees to wear women's underwear; Forcing groups of male detainees to masturbate themselves while being photographed and videotaped; Arranging naked male detainees in a pile and then jumping on them; Positioning a naked detainee on a MRE Box, with a sandbag on his head, and attaching wires to his fingers, toes, and penis to simulate electric torture; Writing "I am a Rapest" (sic) on the leg of a detainee alleged to have forcibly raped a 15-year old fellow detainee, and then photographing him naked; Placing a dog chain or strap around a naked detainee's neck and having a female Soldier pose for a picture; A male MP guard having sex with a female detainee; Using military working dogs (without muzzles) to intimidate and frighten detainees, and in at least one case biting and severely injuring a detainee; Taking photographs of dead Iraqi detainees. During the orgy shards of glass

had left deep bleeding cuts in two of us. Breaking chemical lights and pouring the phosphoric liquid on detainees; Threatening detainees with a charged 9mm pistol; Pouring cold water on naked detainees; Beating detainees with a broom handle and a chair; Threatening male detainees with rape; Allowing a military police guard to stitch the wound of a detainee who was injured after being slammed against the wall in his cell; Sodomizing a detainee with a chemical light and perhaps a broom stick. Using military working dogs to frighten and intimidate detainees with threats of attack, and in one instance actually biting a detainee.

"And even if these allegations are true," the radio personality says, "what people need to understand is that we are in a *war* right now, and *that* means that certain—uh—exceptions must be" and I sort of zone out for a while. "Let's take some calls," he says later, and people either agree or disagree with him.

So the end pages are scrawled solid. This documentation will sit sight unseen, lost in a long row of classics, like the factory-sealed deli meats when they sit at the back of the cooler until we need them or they go bad first but we try to use them anyway. This book, I see, has not been checked out in years, and whoever bothered with it on June 7, 1988, left no mark in the text to indicate if it left him with an opinion, feeling, impres-

sion, or sense. I know that just means he is a good public citizen, respectful of the library, but I wish instead he'd left a note
or tagged a signature, anything to bridge the gulf of years.

But on the other hand the list isn't like unique or really
original. I've seen worse stuff in movies. *The dreams of men,
the seeds of commonwealths, the germs of empires; the horror
and despair in so much bloody flesh, nauseating in part, and
in part very beautiful, and what greatness had not floated on
the ebb of that river into the mystery of an unknown earth!* It
kind of kills me to think about too much. *The fascination
of the abomination—you know.* But I have changes of heart
sometimes. *Imagine the growing regrets, the longing to escape,
the powerless disgust, the surrender, the hate.* Suddenly short
of breath as I imagine someone discovering my list and them
imagining me and what I was thinking as I scribbled. If they
could even know, somehow. *I have never had any aptitude for
what is known as striking a pose.* Or maybe I'm not ashamed;
just really careful. I check the book out and take it home, not
intending to ever bring it back.

Some night:

We're messing around and she starts wishing aloud that
we had some rope to play with. I think my belt, the braided
kind, can suffice. She makes fun of my idea. A couple loops
and twists later there she is, wrists bound behind her, tits
stuck thrust forward. She's surprised, pleased; shakes them a
little. I leave her underwear on and knock her around some,
watching it darken.

I flip her on her back and wave my cock in her face. "No," she says, "not in this bed, my boyfriend was just in this bed." That's part of it, I guess. I untie her after a while. She's finishing me off. I'm on my back, she's got a hand on my cock more or less like you'd hold a joystick. In my head I'm sort of flashing on some video games I've played. When the jizz arcs, some splatters the wall. "Goddamnit," she says, then: "Well, you wrecked your fucking shirt, too."

Once more with feeling, one of us says, and the other thinks this is just so funny.

My walk home:

When it's very cold and I hock up and spit a good one there's this blast of condensed breath that explodes out like a wintry comet behind the launch of saliva and phlegm and I think of what I think tracer bullet trails look like—every fifth round—and how it would be to have a gun that fired tracers, or a reason to have a gun that fired tracers. Yeah, that's it, what I'm really after: not the gun, but the reason for having it. But right now it isn't even cold so I guess I'm imagining that part too, and just spitting.

A different day:

Brendan is doubled over, laughing or pretending to laugh. Waving his arms around. Some theatrical skater bullshit. He puts gloves on, makes a joke about the meat slicer.

Today we are the bookends of a four-person operation,

five if you include the girl who works the register, who is hot and mostly ignores us. We both notice when she looks over our way. She takes the orders and the money and a cigarette break every twenty-five minutes. Someone else toasts the bread and applies the meat and cheese I've sliced, another adds the vegetables or whatever else. Jalapeños and honey mustard; low-fat mayonnaise or that orange shit that goes on a Reuben. Brendan wraps them when they're finished, stuffs each in a to-go bag with a slice of pickle wrapped in crinkly waxed paper. What this all translates to is that he and I don't talk much. We are the poles of the production line, separated by the length and specifics of the gourmet sandwich gestation process. Have you had your way today? With who?

Meanwhile:

In Abu Ghraib, which is a dirty building somewhere in a desert, there are former AT RISKs once condemned by every guidance counselor. The grandchildren of immigrants who had the anarchism beaten out of them by cops in Chicago. Ambivalent patriots and even some true believers. And they've all been given loaded weapons and the keys to small rooms containing people that, as a matter of policy, they must learn to hate or else they already do.

I work and I work and I stare at this whirling blade and I think about everything while I slice the

—Ham

Which is roughly the shape of a loaf of bread, though wider and heavier and longer and pink as a boiled baby and is 11 percent water and comes wrapped in this plastic with a red crisscross design on it and when you slice it open a stream of orange-gray liquid spills out and then you pull the whole wrapping off and it makes a wet *huck* noise and a little more liquid spills into the stainless steel washbasin and the blade goes *whir-whir* when you start it up and you have to figure out what's the good number to set the slicer to so that the meat slices are each three-quarters of an ounce. *(Punching, slapping, and kicking detainees; jumping on their naked feet)* and

—Turkey Breast

I think of that one soldier, the girl, with the cig on her lip and that smile (thumbs-up!) and I can't help but think if she is so evil or lucky or something else I can't imagine and how the turkey breast is roughly the size and weight of a bowling ball that has been squashed a bit—ovalish—it has a brown skin to simulate having been oven-roasted and it is 15 percent water and when you cut the plastic off the liquid spills out golden-brown and then you need to stick it in the freezer for a while so the water in it freezes *(for the first time I saw her "pink and dark" flesh cooling)* because if you cut it while it's warm the water will run right out of it and leave minuscule paths and caverns through the wide pale center of the shiny wet bird-ball so that when you run it *whiz-whiz-whiz* over the blade it will make slices that fall into your waiting medical-gloved hand as streamers of turkey-ribbon or small piles of turkey-rags because it, like everything, loses coherence in the aftermath of losing essential waters *attaching wires to his fingers, toes, and penis to simulate electric torture* and okay duh it's not like the Iraqis at Abu Ghraib were the first people in history to find themselves naked at the wrong end of a dog leash and

—Roast Beef

maybe what I really need to be thinking about *Placing a dog chain or strap around a naked detainee's neck and having a female Soldier pose for a picture* is what Andrea is thinking or if Will is hitting her and if he is is she thinking about *Threatening male detainees with rape* me and how each time

—Pepperoni

is like a first time: I wake up with her smell on me after dreaming of her smell; I know her body so well I could shop for her but every time she undresses I'm thrilled again to learn what she looks like naked and when she's on her back, knees up, thighs like a foyer, I always find myself wondering despite all previous knowledge how will she taste, how will it be when our slick skins finally press hard and the act and all thoughts about the act meld into some third thing—

She is a magic trick and I am either the magician or the crowd.

•   •   •

My shift ends in the early afternoon but Brendan works till four o'clock so I get to say good-bye to him, passing close in the narrow corridor. If we were both skaters I guess we'd slap fives or I'd hit him in the back of the head for a prank or something. He wraps a steaming steak sandwich in tin foil. "Later," I say and he says yeah, peace, or whatever. Puts the sandwich in a paper bag. Takes it back out and goes, "Ahh fuck, fuck this shit."

A mailman on his lunch break is waiting for the steak sandwich Brendan is doing triage on. Maybe the kid who works the microwave forgot to melt the provolone cheese. It's bad when you forget something, but it's worse if you put the wrong thing on. Like if the guy said no mustard but you doused it and then realized. The whole thing gets junked and you start again, and the mailman just stands there. In the far corner on the shop's big screen, Rumsfeld is being grilled about the torture photos. The boss has closed caption on and the volume off. Anyway it doesn't matter. I'm out the door.

Phone call:

"I think Will knows."

"Knows what? I mean how?"

"You fucking bruised me, is how."

"How can he tell which bruises are his and which are mine?"

"What— Fuck. I don't know. He probably can't. But he thinks something."

"Leave him. I'll be good to you."

"Fuck you."

"No but we could—"

Click.

Numerology:

Class of 2000, that's us. Me, Andrea, Will—one for each zero. They raised us to worship our own greatness, to believe ourselves touched by fortune. Destiny, whatever. They put all their faith in the calendar's promise, that glistening fake-out, and we came of age in time to vote but it turned out to be the one when votes stopped counting, if they ever did, and they sent us off to school and we went and then we finished and there was nowhere left to go. The streets are empty. The air is humid, overripe, stinking. Our dead-end jobs have cut us back to summer hours. Anyone with anywhere else to be is already there. Florida! Goddamn.

Is it any wonder we're going feral?

Andrea is downing a shot of Absolut and I am telling her about Brendan. She puts the empty glass down, goes, "I fucking love skaters, why are they all so fucking hot?" and opens the front door. Porch light spills in. She becomes obscure in a personal cloudbank of Marlboro exhaust. I follow her. "Remember Brian Lumes?" she says, speaking of skaters.

I set us up with a couple more shots.

"And he had that fucking haircut," she says. "The weird long front lock that went down his face and it was like his head was melting." And we used to make so much fun of him but he didn't care because he was probably fucked up on ecstasy or else just stoned.

Andrea takes her shot. I take mine. I guess she got out of whatever it was that Will suspected, or maybe that was just some wild shit he said when they were in a fight about something else. Probably he thinks his girl would never cheat on him, but that it still makes sense for him to call her a whore.

Will:

It's better when she's in a fight with him. She comes over alone and gives me her full attention. I hate Will, obviously, because he has her and because sometimes he hurts her, but he's good to keep at a distance because he can always get the best drugs and because he has her. She doesn't love him but won't consider leaving, so what's the point of fighting him or something? I like to think I could save her if she'd let me but Will and I are her two worlds and she mostly keeps us apart. I don't even know if she likes him. I try to imagine them sitting on a loveseat, wearing their socks but not their shoes, watching a sitcom, twirling angel hair pasta up from blue bowls, and my mind goes to static, a bright blank seething wall.

We weren't always like this, but whatever we used to be is hard to focus on from where I'm standing, like trying to imagine what the last guy who checked out the Conrad book was thinking or the credit card guy's eyes getting stung shut by sweat so he doesn't get a decent enough look at me to hail a cop and report the stolen radio. It may even be somehow that whatever Will does to her makes her want what she wants with me—a thought I can hardly stomach. What she and I have is a trust thing, roughly.

Andrea and I are in facing chairs, holding ashtrays, and for a weird minute I start wishing she weren't here so I could be reading or on the net trying to score more photos (because I think there are secrets to be learned, and that I can learn them, even if the secrets don't want to be learned, and I love to learn secrets and then own the truth) but then my attention snaps back either to whatever Andrea's saying or to the shooting-star tattoos. One per hip. Andrea swears the left one is a little fucked up because the tattoo guy did it second and by that time the Vicodin Will gave her had worn off so she was flinching. This is bullshit because Andrea doesn't flinch. Period. Do anything. And besides, I don't see the flaw. I see twin comets, dive-bombing like predatory birds past the waterline at the rim of her tight low-rise black jeans, the arc of the stars' descent such that if her body is the universe the galaxial collision must blaze in the far astral reach of her hidden cunt.

Across the street, through a window with a gauzy curtain, I see the silhouettes of some couple lost in whatever makes them unique to each other. Andrea gives voice to her boredom. There is noise like a party coming from the other direction. We decide to go and see.

●   ●   ●

Getting lucky:

Kids smoke cigarettes and dope. It's a little apartment building that started life as a large house. My friend Melissa lives on the bottom right. Somebody's big brother or sister must live here. I take Andrea's hand just because I want to; because I just want to. I say something about keeping her close to me, not losing her in the crowd, which she ignores. And pulls her hand free. A boy in a shadow says something about her being sexy and I turn toward him and he turns away.

Brendan's with some friends. A tall, unattractive girl in an expensive black miniskirt and red bra hurtles down the stairs, barely keeping upright, screaming the name of a person she needs to fucking talk to right-a-fucking-way. The disinterested skaters on the lawn tell her that guy ain't here, and to lift her skirt up. Negotiations begin. Soon a tall kid, mildly Hispanic, has the shirtless girl pinned on the grass, off to a side. Brendan is a particular kind of embodied dream, hitching his pants up and sidling toward us, mumbling something like "Hey, it's the guy that cuts the meat yeah hey" and puts out a hand that I slap five. The crack of palm on palm reverberates in my head. Keep it together, hold your shit.

"Lame party," I say.

Brendan: "Huh?" From closer up, he's clearly zoned.

"Come with us to my place," I say. "It's just over there," and I point around the corner. "We'll, uh, chill out or whatever." Brendan looks across his scatter of friends, some of them drinking bottles of domestic beer, others presumably loaded some other way.

"Well," he says evasively, but comes. Bops his head a little, hearing some dumb internal music we probably wouldn't be into. I let go of Andrea. Nobody talks. We round the corner.

One time:

I'm reading *Story* at the sandwich shop on my break and sort of watching Brendan in the background. I'm underlining something *(these orgasms were as different from normal climaxes as, say, the mirth of savage Africans from that of Occidentals)* but then it gets busy and I'm back on the clock, so I grab a packet of sugar from a little dish of them and stick it in the book for a bookmark, and then later, I'm reading to Andrea *(It is not astonishing that the bleakest and most leprous aspects of a dream are merely an urging)* and I get this idea about if we could be sweet for a change so I tell her I'm going to sugar her cunt down and lick it clean. I pour out the contents of the packet and lean in. For a moment I'm consumed by the genius conflict of her salts with the sweetness, but then a foul taste takes over and I gag badly. I choke. She props herself up on an elbow, nipples wilting, and reads the torn empty packet: "You asshole," she says. "The pink ones aren't sugar they're Sweet'N Low."

We get to my place. I run in to use the bathroom but stop to put on CNN real quick. Footage of congressmen. But they're not showing the pictures. I have all the pictures, I don't need them to be broadcast in order to see them, but it makes me feel better to see them on TV. Even though the good parts are blurred out. Somehow, the broadcast makes everything okay. *Sodomizing a detainee with a chemical light and perhaps a broom stick*, I think to myself. *Using military working dogs to frighten and intimidate detainees with threats of attack, and in one instance actually biting a detainee.* I don't need the TV to tell me the list. I have memorized the list. I have collected all the photos. I shut the TV off.

Or:

On a different day if I'm by myself, I might take the Bataille and Conrad books and put them side by side, maybe break the two spines trying to make their words merge—but they won't. You can get drunker, push harder—they just dry rub. So you turn back to that desert that is offered to you, glowing.

I think of the cool hum-whine of the meat slicer and of the similar noise my computer makes. Pictures only show you. They don't let you *feel* it. And I feel it. Or want to how badly?

These are glimpses of what I'm thinking about as I light another cigarette off Andrea's, offer one to Brendan, which he accepts, dodge the dirty look she gives me. We sip strong gin and tonics. Andrea and I are both curious to see what Brendan is capable of. I know she likes the idea of Brendan. And the physique. She's probably wondering if he'll let us hit him.

I grip his shoulder in a guy way, briefly, but dig into the muscle to really feel it, like testing a melon or a cut of meat at the grocery store. There's some give, then tautness—that's him flexing. More or less what I had imagined he felt like, but it's good to know for sure. For a second I'm convinced that he's figured us out, but he downs the last of his gin and tonic, hands me the empty glass, eyes Andrea. "Have another drink," I say, and he laughs.

I go to the kitchen and pour another round, but insist we all also take a shot, and Brendan visibly crosses some line, so I push him backward and he falls into Andrea, all of us laughing, and she says we should think of something fun to do.

Me and Andrea have a little aside while Brendan is drunkenly browsing the stuff on my bedroom walls. Or maybe that's him trying to stay standing, or maybe that's him on the bed. I want to try Conrad. She thinks this is insane, even cheesy, which I think is unfair, but you can't culture a pissy drunk, so it's old Bataille. We sit down in a little row on the edge of my bed, Brendan, our Marcelle, in the middle. We're basically holding him upright.

I grew up very much alone, and as far back as I recall I was frightened of anything sexual . . . and the next day there were such dark rings around my eyes . . . so bluntly craved any upheaval . . . I ought to say, nevertheless, that we waited a long time . . . Simone's ass, raised aloft, did strike me as an all-powerful entreaty . . . Only now did we tear loose from our extravagant embrace to hurl ourselves upon a self-abandoned body . . . Marcelle, who no longer hid anything but her sobs . . .

I steal peeks of what is going on over there, getting hot myself, waiting for Andrea to make a move. She takes Brendan's hand and places it on top of my crotch, where it sort of strokes while I keep reading—*We understood one another, Simone and I, and we were certain . . . I ought to say that we were all very drunk and completely bowled over by what was going on . . . "You're totally insane, little man," she cried, "I'm not interested—here, in a bed like this, like a housewife and mother! I'll only do it with Marcelle!"*—then Andrea and I clasp hands around Brendan's cock, which at some point came out of his pants, which are in a bunch at his feet. Then she pulls her hand back. She stands up. I grab her by her wrist and swing her back toward the bed. She goes easy and sort of gets flung at Brendan, who is mostly insensible. She lands in a sexy sprawl, knocking him backward, pressing his cock between their bodies. I pull her back upright, holding her against my body, pulling her shirt up and her bra down. "Nice," the skater says, or really croaks, and she kicks him hard. I knock her down, tear at her clothing. It comes off easily enough, without her help I mean, and I'm glad to feel the wet heat radiating off her as I get her pants off. The underwear is expensive, frilly, and this disappoints or provokes me. When she's naked the tattoos lose their enormous power, and for a long terrible moment I realize (again) that this was better to dream about than to live through and I wish that it was over or that I would die suddenly but I force myself to unrealize that thing so it is no longer a fact or a truth but just one more of the *jewels flashing in the night of time* and force her facedown so I can take her from behind while Brendan half-heartedly grabs at my balls and after I pull out he licks me clean, and I think of *Writing "I am a Rapest" (sic) on the leg of a detainee alleged to have forcibly raped a 15-year old fellow detainee, and then photographing him naked* and I want him to have her, too, but he can't get very hard so I sort of guide him in and out for a little while but then give up *and having accepted the situation without even trying to fathom the mystery* we curl up together at the far end of my bed and he passes out while Andrea wipes herself off and gathers her clothing and I watch her get dressed and I watch her as she walks out of my bedroom and I let her go, but then I sort of realize something and jump up from the bed and run after her and catch her in the living room, right by the front door, which is open, the doorway frames us and the yellow porch light makes a sickly bath, the collar of her shirt all stretched to ruin and her face puffy and I'm naked and who knows what I look like and I say, "What just happened?" even though *by a sort of shared modesty, Simone and I had always avoided talking about the most important objects of our obsessions* and my voice sounds fucked up, like it's too flat or maybe too emotional, so I try to put it another way: "That was what you wanted, right?"

WHISTLE THROUGH YOUR TEETH
AND SPIT

Riot's moseying down East Fourth Street, past the KGB Bar, eating a burrito he found wrapped in tin foil in a garbage can at the corner of Third Avenue. He's filthy and thin. The burrito's beef so he doesn't want to be seen with it, because even though he's personally freegan the crowd at the benches in Tompkins Square includes several hardcore vegans who will all give him shit, and frankly he isn't in the mood. So he's dawdling. Not like he's in some hurry.

Riot wears an eye patch and a grungy white leather jacket he found in a giveaway box at the Bowery Mission and subsequently augmented—in Sharpie, it should go without saying—so his favorite bands (Black Flag, Choking Victim, etc.) are represented up and down the sleeves. The whole back of the thing is given over to one single statement: 9/11 WAS A

REICHSTAG, a subject that he is prepared to talk about for as long as you are prepared to listen, and then some. Actually, it's pretty convincing until he gets into this tired shit about the International Jewish Conspiracy. Yeah man, we know *all* about the Israel connection.

Now he's at the southwest corner of East Fourth and First. He finishes the burrito, balls the foil up in his palm, tosses the ball into a green metal garbage can identical to the can he pulled the meal out of mere minutes ago, crosses First against the light, causing several cab drivers and one tricked-out SUV to honk at him. At these receding vehicles he flips birds—one after another until each is accounted for. The light changes, he crosses north on Fourth against *that* light, and then starts east again. When he hits Avenue A he turns back north and when he gets to St. Mark's Place he decides that maybe he still doesn't really want to go hang out with the kids in the park. What he really wants—check that, *needs*—is a bathroom.

Is it possible that the burrito, so recently regarded as a godsend, is in fact to blame?

"Hey bro," he says to an older woman leading a wheezing pug. "Could you help me out real quick? I'm trying to take the train out to the island and see my grandma, but I'm a little short." The woman walks on without regarding him. Now his insides are clenching. He feels sweat form on his brow. The street is bereft of pedestrians, save a few people who look too much like himself to be worth approaching.

Wait.

There's one pocket he didn't check. The little one where he sometimes . . . yes! It's paper. A fiver, in fact. Well glory be.

Tim, thirty-one, was just starting a relationship with Kim, when his long-time friend Natalie, twenty-nine, told him she was maybe finally ready to give him and her the real chance they'd both always sort of known he secretly believed they had. So even though the Kim thing looked promising, he broke it off. He is questioning this decision now, because after about six weeks with Natalie it's becoming clear that there was a lot more emphasis on that "maybe" than he had counted on. In fact, if he's not mistaken, he's actually being broken up with by her right now. She's in the middle of a long monologue about how they never should have risked something so precious and rare as the true connection they've always had, and how some things are better than sex, even if it isn't "cool" to say so, and what they need to do now is start figuring out how to get back to the way things were before. Let's be adults about this.

They're in her bed; it's Saturday morning—about ten thirty. Her apartment is on East Ninth Street between C and D.

Tim's nodding his head like he agrees with her. He doesn't. He thinks they actually meant what they said while they were having sex last night: an unexpected call and response of I Love You and I Love You, Too.

Tim can't remember who said it first and who replied. If

he could only know that, he's certain he'd have the key to the whole situation. At the very least he'd like to talk about the fact that it *was* said, but he can't take the chance of saying "we" and then being told it was he who went first and that she was merely caught up in the moment, or worse, being nice. On the other hand if it was Natalie who said it first then maybe she's waiting—secretly begging—for him to hold her to her words and save them both. Natalie, you are scared and that's okay. Natalie, stop sabotaging the best thing that's ever happened to either of us.

Tim: "Yeah, I guess you're right," and related platitudes.

God, he's as bad as she is. Natalie can tell. In the larger karmic whatever sense, they totally deserve each other, or they would if they didn't each deserve abject loneliness even more. Everyone gets what they've got coming, and when they don't that just means that the injustice of undeserved suffering is in fact the very thing that's deserved. Christ. This meta-analytical shit chatters away in Natalie's head all day. She's so smart that it's actually disturbing—or else makes perfect sense—that she doesn't have health insurance because she won't stay at any job long enough to qualify. Or that she gets into these situations with guys like Tim. Oh, *here* we go, start ripping on him. All he ever did was whatever you wanted.

Yeah, well who says you can't hold *that* against someone?

In case you can't tell, Natalie's having a little episode, but in her head of course. Real-life Natalie is sitting quietly in bed, speech long finished, sheet pulled up to her neck and naked beneath it, weirding Tim out with her silence, though it's safe to say he wouldn't be any less weirded out if he could somehow know what she's thinking.

Tim's dressed now, standing at the door. Natalie's in a robe. It looks soft, well worn: comfort clothes. They have a quick, awkward good-bye kiss. It should feel like the end of something. It doesn't, but it's not exactly a beginning either. It just is, and then a second later it just was. Now Tim's on the street. He should probably go home and get some work done, but fuck it.

Tim does freelance web design and plays in a cover band at a tourist trap in the West Village, an overpriced bar-restaurant his friend Ted owns. He's not saving at all, but he's been making rent every month and doing okay, which is more than he could have said not too long ago.

At Summer of Love, it's always 1969, even though everyone knows the Summer of Love was '67. Or, more to the point: precisely because nobody knows. Tim is a great guitar player, which is why he gets to play lead on Tuesday, Thursday, and Saturday nights, when Summer of Love has the Grateful Dead on the main stage, i.e., the dining room. They play two sets a night, like the real band used to, and they use authentic vintage set lists—except for dressing up, they make every attempt to re-create the original show. Of course Tim usually wears ruddy corduroys and a black tee shirt, so he actually *is* dressed up like Garcia, albeit nineties Garcia, but when people think Grateful Dead they think tie-dye so nobody gets the reference, or if anyone does it's just like, *Okay, so?*

Tim's favorite coffee shop is at the corner of Ninth and Avenue A. It's called Harry Smith, and if that doesn't tell you everything you need to know about the place odds are it isn't for you, though try explaining *that* to the recent influx of yuppies. You can always tell an outsider because they call it Harry Smith*'s*, as in, "Hey do you want to come meet me? Where are you? I'm like a block off St. Mark's at Harry Smith's, yeah, it's like a coffee place. It's a little smelly but I think they'll let you plug in your laptop."

That's what Tim hears a girl saying into her cell phone as he opens the door and steps in.

They used to have a strict no-phone policy here. Whoever was working would walk up to you and ask nicely, once. If you gave them any shit it was the boot. Those were back in the days when a cell phone was considered a rude luxury, an ostentatious marker of caste. The no-phone sign is still up, but the rule hasn't been enforced in years. The future is whatever you submit to. Someone should write *that* on a wall.

The shop's heritage is scribbled on its walls in Sharpie, that latter-day chisel, that soot-tipped stick. Above the front door, where in Dante there's that warning about abandoned hope, some prophet—alias unknown—has scribbled PUNX NOT DEAD ITS SLEEPING. And underneath that, in smaller letters, black Sharpie again, but clearly the work of a different hand: EVERYTHING HERE IS THE BEST THING EVER. Tim, passing beneath it, thinks the same thing he thinks every time he enters here: *Good Lord willing and the creek don't rise.*

Is that a prayer or a joke? He isn't sure. It doesn't matter. By the time he stopped knowing what he believed, and later stopped believing in belief, he had been coming here so long there was no question of ever stopping coming here, because it's a place that he knows and where he is known. Tim even worked here for a stretch, in '02, when things got really *really* bad.

A heart-shaped funeral wreath—it's giant—on a stand in the middle of the room. A white sash like a beauty queen's cutting across it. The sash reads: R.I.P. HARRY SMITH.

"The fuck?" he says to Lisa, who started sometime after he quit but has now been here longer than he's ever seen anyone stay. He thinks they even made her manager, though it isn't the kind of place you'd think of as *having* a manager. Tim sizes her up, as if for the first time, as if he isn't in here four, five times a week for the last like eight years. Lisa is a thickset twenty-something with streaks of bright pink in her chopped-at-the-ears hair and a pair of seriously inviting green eyes.

"Tell me everything," he says. "Make this okay."

"It sort of is. I don't know. I mean business has been all right, like the numbers and stuff. Lionel and Sadie aren't selling or anything, they're just sort of—tired, of this, I guess, business model. They're going to sort of re-do it like a family place. Like where they could bring their own kids, you know? But they're keeping on everyone who wants to stay, or I think they are. I mean, I'm staying. I don't know, we'll see how it goes, I guess."

Tim has known Lionel and Sadie a long time. Actually, Tim knew Sadie before she even met Lionel, though they never talk about *those* days anymore. He remembers when their first kid was born, the boy, and then the girl came along. He was happy for them, settling down, getting the things they wanted out of life, but it never occurred to him that their lives might ever impact his own. (Of course, their livelihood is his second home and they also employed him, but as far as he's concerned that's a whole other thing.) Tim doesn't like to think of Harry Smith as having had an initial business model, much less a new one. It's always felt more like a public resource—a state park, say—than a business.

Again, this is coming from someone who *worked* here.

Lisa hands Tim the iced chai soy latte that became his new drink two years ago when his trademark double red eyes started leaving him too shaky and heart-palpitated to read the alt weeklies.

Lisa again: "Hey, there's a line forming behind you and they're not regulars, so they don't think this is cute, but listen: we're having a closing party a week from tonight. For just the staff and the, uh, friends of the store or whatever. You should come."

Well that's something, anyway. A party. Tim takes his drink over to the brown couch, where there's a spot open next to Jana, whose name is pronounced as if it started with a Y. She's olive-skinned with a cute nose that goes out just a smidge too far to be as cute as it could be, and a dark pixie haircut that's either brushed to look unkempt or actually is. She wears dark tank tops that favor her smallish breasts without being too showy about it, and black jeans with one of those belts with the double row of metal pyramid studs. They've been friendly with each other for however long she's been coming to Harry Smith. Tim can't remember the first time he saw her but he knows he's got seniority, patron-wise, which makes sense because at thirty-one he's probably what—five, six years older than she is? They're about on op-posite ends of a long trip to college. That's another way of saying she was still in high school the year he thought he was going to get famous, and probably she was taking The Bible as Literature for a funky junior elective while he was work-ing here.

"So what do you think of all this?" Tim says to Jana, gesturing at the wreath. He wonders who ordered it, if it was Lionel and Sadie or one of the other regulars. (Every regular secretly believes he is *the* regular, most cherished and be-loved, so if someone else was told about this before him, who and why?)

"What's to think?" Jana says. "Everyone sells out, appar-ently. This city is a dead fucking husk."

Riot opens the front door. Figure he's about Tim's age, might even be older. With homeless people it's hard to tell. He holds the door for a bottle blond in end-of-season-sale designer wear. A case in point for Jana if there ever was one.

"After you, miss," Riot says with an exaggerated courtesy that is really leering. It's amazing the girl doesn't bolt, she's so obviously icked out by him. Time was, Tim thinks, a girl like that wouldn't set foot in a place like this. These days, she probably lives around the corner, pays four figures for a fifth-floor walkup, and when the deliveryman brings the Thai food she tips him $2 instead of $3 because she always remembers what Daddy said about a penny saved and a penny earned.

Lisa sees Riot and the first thing she says is "No."

"Hey c'mon man c'mon," he says, "I got money today. I just gotta use the john first."

"No way."

The girl Riot held the door for has found her friend. Not surprisingly, it's the girl who was on the cell phone when Tim walked in.

"All right all right," Riot says. He orders a coffee and throws his five on the counter.

Lisa isn't sure what to do. What she'd like to do is throw Riot out on his ass. He's been banned for life from this place more times than anyone can count, but here's the thing: if she throws him out he'll stand in the street and scream about fascism and panhandle passersby and generally make a scene until somebody—probably Lisa—calls the cops and then they'll show up and then there'll be *that* scene going down out front. What she's thinking is that maybe if she just serves him, he'll be cool. Who knows? Stranger things have happened at this place, though not many.

She takes his money and turns to pour the coffee. Riot takes the bathroom key from the counter and heads for the back.

Tim and Jana have been silently watching all this go down. Tim's been trying to decide whether he should get involved: maybe tell Lisa to cool off; maybe tell Riot he can have a dollar if he goes outside. Who knows what Jana thinks of these people and all this? She's sipping a black coffee. Tim wonders if it's got sugar at least. He says, "Well, you're coming to the party, right?"

"Who wants to celebrate death?" Jana says.

A few minutes go by. They sip their drinks without talking. It occurs to Tim that Riot still hasn't come out of the bathroom. "Hey, Lisa."

"Was thinking the same thing, hon," Lisa says. She shouts: "RIOT! TEN SECONDS AND I KICK THE FUCKING DOOR IN."

Tim laughs and shakes his head. Lisa will *never* last as manager after the place goes bourgeois.

"Four . . . three . . . two . . . OKAY ASSHOLE HERE I COME. YOU BETTER HAVE GODDAMN PANTS ON." Lisa's ready to kick, but the door's not locked. This could be anything.

It isn't.

What's in the toilet is gross (Riot didn't flush) but at least he's not playing with it. Or shooting up or something. In fact, he seems to have forgotten about what's in the toilet altogether. He's got a Sharpie out, is detailing some of his 9/11 theories on the lid of the tank. "People have to know," he tells Lisa. She grabs him by the jacket, sort of hurls him into the hall, hits the flush with her boot.

"All right, asshole," she says. "You're finished. Straight out the door or I'm calling."

"You're just a cog in their machine," Riot says. "Towing the fascist line."

"You know what?" She reaches for the phone. "You're right."

"Fine, okay, shit, Jesus. Put my drink in a to-go cup and I'm out of here."

Tim's from somewhere shitty in the Midwest. He was a good student, growing up, then college was a lot to handle (shrooms, mostly) so he wound up dropping out of Colorado State spring semester freshman year, took some time off, then got into the jazz program at The New School and moved to New York. He even graduated, though barely, since after moving to the city he discovered the then-burgeoning freak-folk scene. Tim knows his old band, Flash Pounce, could have gotten big if they'd stuck with it. They had a legendary live show, every venue wanted to book them. They broke up for the usual reasons: artistic differences and a couple of them got way too into speed and then the trumpet/synth player got engaged, decided to move back to Chicago.

Natalie calls Tim on Tuesday night, technically Wednesday morning. It's about two thirty. He was sleeping, but when she asks if she woke him up he says she didn't. He says he just got home, in a way that he hopes somehow implies he was out on a date.

"It's too bad you're so far away," she slurs. "I miss you."

"I could catch a train, I guess." There are no cabs in the part of Brooklyn where Tim lives.

"No, it's so late."

"Yeah, you're right. So."

"Tim. Listen. Listen. Maybe we could . . . talk?" There's a weird weight on that word. Talk about what? Them? What's left to say? Is she going to break up with him again for good measure?

But he says sure, of course, and she starts talking. Saying the filthiest things, actually, first about what they did over the weekend, then made-up stuff. She describes in torrid, exalting detail all the nasty things they're doing to each other that they're not doing to each other. At some point he realizes she's jerking off. So . . . He should, too—right?

This hand is Natalie's hand.

This hand is Natalie's face, etc.

"Oh fu-uck," she says, and makes some noises in the phone that Tim tries to convince himself he is hearing for the second time this week, though if he's going to be honest with himself (he's not) she sounds way more excited right now than she did when they were together in person, though it's not exactly a revelation that everyone's their own best lover. Who knows what you want better than you do? (Little joke.) Anyway, he's been on the verge himself for, say, four or five minutes now. What's he holding back for? There's no etiquette when she's not really there.

It's Saturday night. They're doing 4/30/77, which means no bluesy Pig Pen–era stuff, plus the country tunes are jazzier and slowed way down. A '71 "Friend of the Devil" is a three-minute up-tempo ramble. A '77 "Friend of the Devil" is two, three times as long and you sing it like a dirge, as much despair as you'd bring to singing "St. James Hospital" or something. And then "Terrapin Station," a spacey epic about which the less said the better.

For one last encore they do "Touch of Grey," the Grateful Dead's only number-one hit, even though it didn't get written until 1980-something; officially released in '87. No matter what show they're doing, they always do last encore "Touch of Grey." It's house policy.

Luckily, the tourist crowd goes back to their hotels early. Maybe they all have matinee tickets for tomorrow. Tim's out of there by midnight. Pretty nice out, actually. He walks from the one village to the other. He's almost there when his phone buzzes. Any guesses who this is gonna be?

"Hey, where are you, are you home?"

"No, actually I'm on my way to a party near your place. You want to come meet me?"

"I don't think that's a good idea, Tim."

"Why do you keep saying that? I want to see you. You want to see me."

"I liked what we did the other night."

Silence from Tim.

"Didn't you like that?" she says. "Wasn't I good?"

How to even begin to approach answering that question? Maybe say, *You* weren't actually anything. *You* weren't there, *I* wasn't there. Or: this is *too weird*. He could say all those things right now. He could say what he really feels and see where it gets him.

"Yeah no I mean yeah you were good. It was good."

"Call me when you get home, Tim. I mean if you want to."

At the party, two guys Tim recognizes but doesn't know by name are talking music. The one with the beard is saying to the one in the fedora that the proof of Will Oldham being the new Bob Dylan is in the way he adapts his own songs for live performance.

"Listen to *Summer in the Southeast* and compare that version of 'I Send My Love to You' to the one on *Days in the Wake*. Then go listen to the *Blood on the Tracks* 'Shelter from the Storm' and compare it to the live version on *Hard Rain*."

"Yeah, and what am I supposed to be seeing when I do that?"

"When you see it you won't need me to tell you."

"You know," Tim cuts in, "who Dylan says is the best interpreter of his songs?"

Fedora: "Who?"

Tim: "No guesses?"

Beard: "Hendrix?"

Tim: "Jerry Garcia."

One of them: "You're fucking joking."

The other one: "And it's not funny."

Tim, smiling—it's the stone truth—plucks a beer from the cooler planted next to the register, then he wanders out back.

Surprise, surprise.

"Oh so what?" Jana says to him. "I was bored."

"Hey, nobody said anything," Tim says. "Have you been here long?"

Now they're getting to know each other, and isn't this nice? No spark, exactly. This isn't going to be like one of those things where the one girl breaks your heart and then you meet this other one and realize it was all meant to be: good things to those who wait, etc. Actually, Jana's kind of a bitch. He's telling her about Summer of Love and she's practically doubled over laughing at him.

"I think I'll head in for another drink," Tim says, hoping she takes his implied meaning, which is, I am *so* done talking to you. But then for some reason he says, "Want me to grab you one?" and she says "Yeah, that'd be great, thanks." First he's thinking, Jesus what did I say that for? But then he starts thinking how if she took him up on the offer she maybe isn't having such a bad time with him, and if she's not having a bad time maybe he isn't either.

Jana actually isn't thinking about Tim one way or the other. All she wanted was another beer and another cigarette, and you can't smoke inside, so. But fuck it, this party sucks anyway. She crushes out her smoke, goes in, sees him talking to somebody over by the booze, doesn't bother to say good-bye. She goes out the front door and turns north on Avenue A. About half a block up from Harry Smith she runs into Riot, who is curled up like a child, bawling, in front of some new boutique store. The chain gate is down—it's closed for the night—but you can make out what's in the window. He smells sour. Shitty malt liquor, she bets, not that there's another kind.

Riot: "fuhuhuhuck."

Jana: "Hey, man, are you okay?" He says nothing, points straight up at the window. It's the cover of *Stations of the Crass* silk-screened onto the front of a black pre-stressed designer tee shirt. Nothing so gauche as an advertised price but Jana figures, what—$120? She thinks of herself in middle school, standing in line at the Hot Topic at the mall in a suburb outside Philly, buying a red shirt emblazoned with Che's face. They commodified her emotions, sold her own rebellion back to her before she even knew it for what it was. Is that better or worse than the post-ironic self-aware sellout-sophisticate garb on display here? Fuck it, it's all one big Disneyland, and this is a fallen world. No place to hide your faith for safekeeping.

Or maybe the lesson is that faith is a perishable good, cannot be saved for later, is nothing if it is not action in the world. That sounds like a protest sign, or a long-winded bumper sticker.

But is it *true*?

"Come on," she says to Riot. "Buck up, and let's go scrounging."

After Tim realizes Jana's gone he pounds the beer that was hers. He means to pound the second one too, but gives himself the hiccups with the first one and has to stand there and wait it out. Then he joins some conversation already in progress. A guy with a compass rose tattoo on his right hand is saying, "That's actually one of my favorite things about tattoos—that they make the body seem less sacred. The body *isn't* sacred. People should see things for what they are."

Some drunk asshole calls the room to order and makes a toast Tim wishes he'd thought to make, then a bottle of Jack gets passed around and Tim has a big swig of that and then he feels sort of sick so he goes back outside—to the front this time—to have a smoke and calm his stomach. Jana and Riot walk past, carrying a metal post like stop signs are mounted on. "We found it in a Dumpster on Second," she says to Tim as they pass by. Avenue or street? he wonders. Not that it matters. How long ago did he hang up with Natalie? Either half as long or twice as long as it feels like, so figure an hour. He lurches across the street, almost gets nailed by a cab in the process, doesn't even turn when he hears the rebuke of the horn. He walks through Tompkins Square Park, sits down on Natalie's stoop, digs his phone out of his pocket and calls. The door of the building is painted metal, cold against his forehead when he leans.

Just when he thinks she's not going to answer.

Natalie: "Oh, hey."

"Hey, are you still awake? I'm home."

ACKNOWLEDGMENTS

I wish to extend my gratitude to the editors of the magazines, journals, Web sites, and anthologies in which several of these stories were first published and/or reprinted.

The following people have been and are my teachers, editors, first-readers, confidants, employers, family members, and friends. I hope you all know how grateful I am for the vital roles you play in my life, to say nothing of the life of this book.

THANK YOU: Danielle Benveniste, Blake Butler, Dennis Cooper, Elliott David, Mark Doten, David Gates, Fran Gordon, Bill Hayward, Gordon Lish, Peter Masiak, Amy McDaniel, Charles McNair, Amanda Peters, Robert Polito, Jeremy Schmall, Michael Signorelli, Eva Talmadge, Maggie Tuttle; my parents, and my sister, Melanie; the Taylor, Starkman, and Goldner families.